Other Books by Harriet Steel

Becoming Lola

Salvation

City of Dreams

Following the Dream

The Inspector de Silva Mysteries

Trouble in Nuala

Dark Clouds over Nuala

Offstage in Nuala

Fatal Finds in Nuala

Christmas in Nuala

Passage from Nuala

Short stories

Dancing and other stories

AN INSPECTOR DE SILVA MYSTERY

ROUGH TIME IN NUALA

HARRIET STEEL

MYS
STEEL

Author's Note and Acknowledgements

Welcome to the seventh book in my Inspector de Silva mystery series. Like the earlier ones, this is a self-contained story but, wearing my reader's hat, I usually find that my enjoyment of a series is deepened by reading the books in order and getting to know major characters well. With that in mind, I have included thumbnail sketches of those featuring here who took a major part in previous stories. I have also reprinted this introduction, with apologies to those who have already read it.

A few years ago, I had the great good fortune to visit the island of Sri Lanka, the former Ceylon. I fell in love with the country straight away, awed by its tremendous natural beauty and the charm and friendliness of its people who seem to have recovered extraordinarily well from the tragic civil war between the two main ethnic groups, the Sinhalese and the Tamils. I had been planning to write a detective series for some time and when I came home, I decided to set it in Ceylon in the 1930s, a time when British Colonial rule created interesting contrasts, and sometimes conflicts, with traditional culture. Thus, Inspector Shanti de Silva and his friends were born.

I owe many thanks to everyone who helped with this book. My editor, John Hudspith, was, as usual, invaluable and Jane Dixon Smith designed another excellent cover for me, as well as doing the elegant layout. Praise from the many readers who told me that they enjoyed the previous books in this series and wanted to know what Inspector de Silva and his friends got up to next encouraged me to keep going. Above all, heartfelt thanks go to my husband, Roger, without whose unfailing encouragement and support I might never have reached the end.

Apart from well-known historical figures, all characters in the book are fictitious. Nuala is also fictitious although loosely based on the hill town of Nuwara Eliya. Any mistakes are my own.

**Characters who appear regularly in the
Inspector de Silva Mysteries.**

Inspector Shanti de Silva. He began his police career in
Ceylon's capital city, Colombo, but, in middle age, he married and accepted a promotion to inspector in charge of
the small force in the hill town of Nuala. Likes: a quiet
life with his beloved wife; his car; good food; his garden.
Dislikes: interference in his work by his British masters;
formal occasions.

Sergeant Prasanna. In his mid-twenties, married with a
baby daughter, and doing well in his job. Likes: cricket and
is exceptionally good at it.

Constable Nadar. A few years younger than Prasanna and
less confident. Married with two boys. Likes: his food;
making toys for his sons. Dislikes: sleepless nights.

The British:

Jane de Silva. She came to Ceylon as a governess to a
wealthy colonial family and met and married de Silva a few
years later. A no-nonsense lady with a dry sense of humour.
Likes: detective novels, cinema, and dancing. Dislikes:
snobbishness.

Archie Clutterbuck. Assistant government agent in Nuala and as such, responsible for administration and keeping law and order in the area. Likes: his Labrador, Darcy; fishing; hunting big game. Dislikes: being argued with; the heat.

Florence Clutterbuck. Archie's wife, a stout, forthright lady. Likes: being queen bee; organising other people. Dislikes: people who don't defer to her at all times.

William Petrie. Government agent for the Central Province and therefore Archie Clutterbuck's boss. A charming exterior hides a steely character. Likes: getting things done. Dislikes: inefficiency.

Lady Caroline Petrie. His wife and a titled lady in her own right. She is a charming and gentle person.

Doctor David Hebden. Doctor for the Nuala area. He travelled widely before ending up in Nuala. Unmarried and hitherto, under his professional shell, rather shy. Likes: cricket. Dislikes: formality.

Emerald Watson. She arrived in Nuala with a touring British theatre company and decided to stay. She's a popular addition to local society, especially where Doctor Hebden is concerned. Her full story is told in *Offstage in Nuala*.

Charlie Frobisher. A junior member of staff in the Colonial Service. A likeable young man who is tipped to do well. Likes: sport and climbing mountains.

CHAPTER 1

Carefully, he positioned himself close to the sixteenth green at the Royal Nuala Golf Club. Satisfied that he was hidden from the sight of any golfers on or near the green, but still able to have a good view of them, he settled down to wait. Surely, even an indifferent golfer like Bernard Harvey would come along soon.

Ten minutes went by; he rolled his shoulders to ease the tension in them and heard the bones crack. Where the hell was Harvey? Perhaps he'd given up. He looked at his watch. He was getting into risky territory, but it might be a long time, if ever, that a chance like this came up again.

At last, Bernard Harvey's short, stocky figure, rendered even bulkier by plus-fours and a brown tweed jacket, appeared in the distance. He was heading for the green: his caddy, labouring under the weight of a bulky bag of golf clubs, following behind.

There was no sign of a ball on the green; Harvey's shot must have fallen short. Yes, it had. Harvey stopped and began to fuss about, eyeing the distance and choosing the club he wanted. Eventually, he made his decision. After pausing to tip up the brim of his cream cap and tug at his collar and the Royal Nuala Club tie encircling it, he addressed the ball.

The shot went wide and bounced past the green into the trees, where the jungle rose up in a dense wall of vegetation.

At a peremptory gesture from Harvey, the caddy started to trudge after it. Stealthily, he moved from his position, calculating the direction he should take for their paths to converge.

When he found him, the caddy was bent over, prodding randomly at piles of leaves and muttering to himself. At the rustle of footsteps, he turned. 'I will find it soon, sahib.' He stopped, a look of surprise coming over his face.

'I'm just looking for something myself,' he said to the caddy in a friendly voice. One hand gripped the cord he held behind his back. The rough hemp prickled his skin. 'You carry on.'

'Thank you, sahib. What is it you are looking for? I will search for it at the same time as Sahib Harvey's ball.'

'Nothing valuable, unless you count sentimental value,' the man said, quickly inventing something. 'A pen.'

The caddy turned away, gesturing to the jungle floor. If he thought a pen was an odd thing to mislay in the jungle, he didn't comment. 'I'm afraid it will not be easy to find, sahib. Even harder than Sahib Harvey's ball perhaps.'

He stepped forward, whisking the cord from behind his back. The caddy only had time to let out a muffled cry before it tightened around his neck, cutting off the oxygen to his brain. Tighter still, and the caddy swayed, hands clawing feebly at the cord, then slumped to the ground.

He stepped back and wiped the perspiration from his eyes with his sleeve. He'd better make absolutely sure the caddy didn't live to tell any tales. Hauling him up so that his body rested against the man's own, he put an arm around the caddy's neck, adjusted his grip and jerked sharply. There was a crack. The fellow wouldn't be doing any talking now.

He made his way back to the place where he had started out. Harvey had moved up to the green. He was just in time to see him take a ball from the pocket of his golf bag and drop it close to the edge of the hole. Exchanging his iron for a putter, he lined up and gave the ball a sharp tap. It teetered on the hole's metal rim then dropped in with a soft click. Harvey bent down and fished it out. Quickly, he filled in his score card then cupped his stubby-fingered hands to his mouth.

'Leave that ball where it is now! I'm in a hurry to move on.' For a few moments, he waited for an answer, then started to walk towards the rough.

The man stepped out of the trees. 'Afternoon, Bernard! How's it going? Tricky little hole this one, isn't it?' He gave Harvey a knowing smile.

Harvey bristled. 'No complaints,' he said curtly. 'If it goes on this way, I won't finish much over par. What are you doing up here, anyway? And why are you carrying that thing?' He looked at the golf club in the man's hand. 'You're not dressed for golf. No tie, and that jacket would disgrace a tramp.'

The man looked at the threadbare sleeves of his shabby jacket and shrugged. 'I lost something when I was playing yesterday. I thought it might be somewhere around here.' He indicated the club. 'Brought this in case I needed to beat down any undergrowth.' He glanced along the fairway. 'All alone? A chap needs to be careful, y'know. I heard a rumour someone saw a leopard prowling around this area the other day.'

'Lot of nonsense,' said Harvey stiffly. 'The perimeter fence is sound, and if it isn't, I damn well want to know why. I've put enough money into this place. It's a bad show if I can't get a bit of practice in private when I want it without risking my life.' He consulted his chunky gold watch. 'Time's getting on. Looks like I'll have to go and find my blasted caddy.'

'Looking for a lost ball, is he?'

Harvey shook his head. 'Blighter asked if he could go and relieve himself in the bushes. Must have a bladder like a bloody elephant.'

An enigmatic smile played on the man's face. 'Perhaps the leopard got him after all.'

'Most amusing.'

Harvey stumbled off into the rough and disappeared into the trees, shouting for his caddy. Briefly, he waited before following him. Everything was going according to plan, but the job wasn't over yet. His gut roiled.

The caddy lay on the ground where he'd left him, the cord that had strangled him still around his neck. Harvey stood over him, a perplexed expression on his pallid, glistening face. 'What the hell's been happening here?' he blustered.

With a hiss, wood and steel sliced the air. At the club's first impact on the back of his skull, Harvey cried out. Twisting to face his attacker, he raised his hands to his head in a futile attempt to ward off the next blow. An indistinct plea gurgled from his lips as he spat out blood and broken teeth. The club came down again and again, until he ceased to struggle and lay motionless.

The man tossed the club down and doubled over. His chest heaved; the trees around him swam before his eyes. A long moment passed before he recovered sufficiently to kneel beside Harvey's body and feel for a pulse, but even then, his hands refused to stop shaking.

The heat of the jungle was unbearably oppressive, now more than ever. Sweat poured off him, drenching his shirt and dripping saltwater into his eyes. He struggled out of the old jacket and loosened his collar. That was better. Trying to ignore the stench of blood, faeces, and urine that rose from Harvey's body, he took a few deep breaths.

Gradually, the shaking lessened. His long fingers probed Harvey's neck, found the carotid artery and remained there, waiting for a sign of life. Nothing.

The man squinted at the sun, still half hidden by the tree canopy. In an hour or so, it would be at its height. He didn't have long to cover his tracks. With a grunt of pain, he got to his feet. Every bone in his body ached from the force he had needed to exert, but he must get that damned golf bag of Harvey's off the green. He didn't want anyone spotting it before he'd had time to clean up.

He glanced in the direction of the dead caddy. Simply a case of being in the wrong place at the wrong time. Just as well he was much slighter in build than Harvey and had been easy to overpower. He'd already decided what to do with him: not a pleasant task, but he'd better get on with it.

After he had dealt with the body, he stripped off the old clothes he wore, washed himself as best as he could using some of the water he'd brought and used what remained to clean the head of the golf club. That done, he donned the clean trousers and jacket he had also taken the precaution of bringing. The discarded clothes were covered in blood. He would have to find some way of disposing of them later.

Dried palm fronds crackled under his feet as he returned to the place where he had left his car. After bundling the blood-stained clothes into a sack, he stowed it and the golf club in the boot, then climbed into the driver's seat and set off. Soon, the course was behind him, and gradually, his grip on the steering wheel slackened. The first part of his plan had gone smoothly. He had nothing to fear.

CHAPTER 2

'May I ask what is so funny?'

Shanti de Silva came into the drawing room from the verandah, where, work over for the day, he had been relaxing in his favourite chair. He crossed to where his wife, Jane, sat at the small table between the windows and looked over her shoulder. The photograph that had made her laugh showed the two of them on holiday in Egypt, mounted on camels, with the Sphinx and the pyramids in the background. Cool and serene, Jane looked as if camel riding was something that she did every day. In contrast, his solar topee was askew, and his expression was far from content. The photograph had been taken by the local guide who had arranged the trip to see the famous sights, using the camera de Silva had bought especially for the holiday. Shortly afterwards, he recalled, his mount had bolted. As if it were yesterday, he remembered the churning sensation in his stomach and the pounding of his heart in the eternity before the beast had been brought under control.

Jane dabbed her eyes with her handkerchief. 'I'm sorry, dear, but it was rather a comical sight. Now that I know you weren't hurt, of course,' she added hastily. 'You really did very well to hang on until the creature came to a stop.'

A rueful smile replaced de Silva's scowl. 'I suppose it could have been worse. The greatest injury was to my pride. But if we go on holiday again, promise me you'll never suggest we do anything else of that kind.'

'I promise.'

Tucking the photograph into the white corners she had gummed onto a page of their holiday album, Jane smoothed it down. 'There; not many left to do now. I want to write captions under each one, but it will keep until tomorrow.'

'Would you like to go out this evening?'

'That would be nice. I hear the film that's on at the cinema this week is good.'

'What film is that?'

'A comedy with Laurel and Hardy.'

'Then let's go.'

'I'll tell the cook to serve an early supper, shall I?'

'An excellent idea.'

The sound of the telephone ringing drifted from the hall. De Silva frowned. 'Were you expecting a call?'

Jane shook her head as she reached for another photograph: this time a view of the desert with the Sphinx in the foreground. 'No, I don't think so. It can't be Florence about the church flowers. We did them yesterday morning.'

A servant came into the drawing room. 'The call is for you, sahib. It is Doctor Hebden.'

De Silva's frown deepened. Why would David Hebden, the local doctor, call him at home? He hoped nothing was wrong. It would be most unfortunate if anything was about to upset the plan he and Jane had only just made.

He nodded to the servant. 'I'll come.'

In the hallway, he put the black Bakelite receiver to his ear and spoke into the mouthpiece. 'Good evening, Doctor Hebden. What can I do for you?'

Hebden cleared his throat. 'I'm afraid we have a problem, de Silva. Can you come up to the golf club?'

'Of course, if it's an urgent matter.'

'Good man. I've already telephoned the Residence, and Charlie Frobisher will be joining us. Archie Clutterbuck's tied up with some important visitors. I'll call Frobisher back and ask him to collect you on his way.'

De Silva scratched his head. Quite apart from the fact it was odd to call him up to the golf club, why was it necessary to involve one of the Residence staff too? 'Can you tell me more?' he asked.

'I'd rather not say too much on the telephone,' said Hebden in a low voice. There was a long pause; de Silva's policeman's instincts prickled. Clearly, something was seriously wrong. He heard Hebden clear his throat again.

'I'm afraid we have a murder on our hands.'

CHAPTER 3

A red MG drew up at the front door. Charlie Frobisher stepped out and came over to where de Silva waited. Regrettably, his and Jane's evening out would have to keep for another time.

'Hello, Inspector. I'm sorry to disturb you like this, but I believe Doctor Hebden's already told you that we have a nasty spot of bother up at the golf club.'

The remark demonstrated a notable British quality, thought de Silva: their unerring ability to minimise drama, even when, in most people's view, the occasion would justifiably merit it. 'No apology is necessary,' he replied. 'It's my job.'

'Good of you to say so.' Frobisher indicated the MG. 'Shall we take my car? I know the way, and it will be quicker to drive to the place where the body was found than to walk from the clubhouse.'

The MG was far less roomy than de Silva's Morris and lower to the ground. He eased himself cautiously into the passenger seat and did his best to arrange his legs in some semblance of comfort. How did Charlie Frobisher, who must be well over six feet tall, manage? The driver's seat was pushed back as far as it would go, but still the young man's knees almost touched the steering wheel.

The car started with a throaty purr, its wheels kicking up dust as they set off.

'Hebden suggested we approach by way of the road that leads to the back of the course,' shouted Frobisher over the noise of the engine and the rush of air through the open window on the driver's side. 'The dead man is one Bernard Harvey, a wealthy local businessman and tea plantation owner. His body was found in the rough near the sixteenth green. There's a gate we can go through that brings us close to there. It used to be used for bringing up supplies to the halfway hut. Members stopped there when they wanted a glass of something to cool themselves down before finishing a round, but it's been abandoned for many years.'

'Who found Mr Harvey's body?' asked de Silva, bracing himself as the MG slewed around a bend.

'Hebden. He was playing a few holes with his fiancée, Emerald Watson, who seems to have taken the discovery calmly enough. But of course, it's not a suitable thing for a lady to witness. Hebden brought her back to the clubhouse when he came to use the telephone.'

The MG turned off the main road and started down a much narrower one where dense jungle closed in on every side. After a short while, they reached a tall metal gate and soon afterwards, a small, nondescript building in a state of extreme disrepair. A black Morris 8 that de Silva recognised as Doctor Hebden's was already parked beside it. Frobisher brought the MG to a stop and jumped out. 'This way, Inspector.'

Exiting the car more gingerly than his companion, de Silva followed him along a path through the trees then over a patch of rough ground that butted up to a neatly mown green. Presumably this place was the "rough" that golfers talked about. The part of the course where one hoped not to send one's ball. A little further on, they went into the trees once again.

David Hebden looked up at their approach.

'Hello, de Silva. Frobisher's filled you in, I take it.'

'To some extent, sir.'

De Silva surveyed Bernard Harvey's dead body. He lay on his right side, one arm flung across his face as if he had been trying to shield himself. It was obvious that he had failed. Where the back of his head should have been, there was only a bloody mush of brains and shattered bone. Blood had soaked into his jacket and splatters of it glistened on the broken branches and leathery straps of dead palm fronds scattered around the body. The scene indicated to de Silva that Harvey's attacker had done his deadly work here, rather than merely using the place as somewhere to dump the body.

'My guess is he was struck down with a golf club,' said Hebden. 'If the attacker was strong, a club could do that much damage if there were multiple blows. Let's hope the poor man was rendered unconscious quickly.'

'How long do you think he's been dead?' asked Frobisher.

'From the condition of the body, I'd say it happened mid-morning.'

'Was it usual for him to play alone?' asked de Silva. 'There's no sign of a partner, I take it.'

'None. I believe Harvey liked to come out by himself to play a few holes on a Friday, but he would have had a caddy with him to carry his bags, and there's no sign of the fellow.'

'Hmm, suspicious,' remarked Frobisher. 'Unless we're about to find another body.'

'Quite.'

De Silva looked around. 'I don't see a golf bag or any clubs,' he said.

'Could've been removed by the killer,' said Hebden. 'Harvey was certainly dressed to play.' He indicated the tweed jacket, plus-fours, thick woollen socks and stout shoes.

With a glance through the trees to where the short grass of the sixteenth green met the rough, de Silva estimated that it was about twenty-five yards away. Far enough for the body not to be noticed from the green. 'What led you to the body, Doctor Hebden?' he asked.

'My dog, Jasper. Emerald was keen we should bring him round with us. She said we mustn't leave him in the car in this heat. I trust him to stay close to me, so he wasn't on his lead, but this time, he disappeared on the scent of something. Poor old Bernard Harvey as it turned out. I called Jasper back, but he just kept on barking until I went to see what the matter was.'

'Lucky he was so persistent, don't you agree?'

'I do, and it's just as well we found Harvey when we did. We have a chance to remove his body without causing a lot of fuss. The course is quiet. That's the main reason Emerald and I were up here. She's only been playing for a few months, and she likes to come out when there aren't too many other people around. I understand the course was closed this morning; something to do with a visit from the new American ambassador who's up from Colombo. Archie Clutterbuck and William Petrie had arranged to play a round of golf with him and someone from his entourage, but tomorrow is bound to be busy.'

He glanced towards the western sky where the sun was rapidly sinking behind the trees. 'Well, what do you want to do, de Silva? We haven't much time left before it gets dark.'

'I'd like to make a search of the area, but I think it will have to wait until morning.'

They all stared at the tangled vegetation around them. 'It won't be easy to spot any clues but worthwhile trying, nevertheless,' he finished.

Hebden nodded. 'It's too late to call the undertakers up tonight. I suggest we move the body to the halfway hut. There should be somewhere there where we can secure it from marauding animals until it can be collected.'

The body of the caddy, in the event he too was dead,

faced a far less respectful fate, thought de Silva. But it couldn't be helped; the chance of finding it in the dark was a million to one.

Saplings had taken root in the halfway hut's brickwork. Vines clambered up to the roof. It was hard to know for how long it had been disused. The jungle didn't take many years to suck an abandoned place into its leafy maw. A dank smell hung over the interior, and bat droppings covered the floor. The door was warped, and the wood at the bottom rotten, but it wasn't a time to be choosy. Frobisher found some dried palm fronds and laid them down as a makeshift bed. They placed Harvey on it and de Silva searched the body briefly. The stench of blood and bat droppings made his nostrils sting as he delved into the pockets of the jacket and plus-fours. They contained a bunch of keys, a crocodile-skin wallet with a thick wad of banknotes in it, a linen handkerchief, a score card, and a stub of pencil. He examined them all but found nothing of interest.

'Harvey's gold watch is still here,' said Frobisher, raising the dead man's limp wrist then replacing it carefully by his side. 'I believe it's worth a considerable amount.'

Doctor Hebden raised an eyebrow. 'As he was fond of mentioning at every opportunity.'

Pulling out a handkerchief, de Silva wiped his hands. 'I think that will have to do for tonight.' He considered the valuables; it wasn't advisable to leave them behind, but he had no proper evidence bags. Wrapping some in his own handkerchief, he used the one Charlie Frobisher offered him for the rest. 'Shall we be on our way, gentlemen?' he asked when he'd finished. 'We'd better stop off at the clubhouse.'

A lump of wood broke off the bottom of the door as Frobisher forced it into the jamb, so between them they piled branches against it to make sure no animal would be able to get into the hut overnight. Frobisher produced a torch and by its beam, they found their way back to the cars through the gathering darkness.

'I suggest you go with Frobisher, de Silva,' said Hebden. When he opened the Morris 8's door, de Silva saw why. A large black Labrador, a juvenile version of Archie Clutterbuck's Darcy, bounded out from the passenger seat and started to run around in circles barking joyfully.

'Jasper! Sit!' boomed Hebden. The canine sleuth sat; pink tongue lolling from his jowls and tail swishing the dusty ground.

'I doubt the boss will want what's happened broadcast,' remarked Frobisher as he and de Silva drove back along the main road behind Doctor Hebden's car. 'Especially as the American ambassador seems very keen to spend more time up here and has billeted himself and his party at the Residence for a few days rather than going back to Kandy with William Petrie.'

Aware that their mutual boss, Archie Clutterbuck, the assistant government agent for the Hill Country, had a fear of scandal, de Silva nodded. Archie was bound to be on edge if the visitors were important enough for his own superior, William Petrie, the government agent, to join them. It would be embarrassing to have a murder cast a cloud over the occasion.

'Of course, a few key people will have to be told,' Frobisher went on. 'The committee, naturally. Apart from the boss, who's our captain, there's Mark Brodie, the club secretary. Tom Duncan is vice-captain, and David Llewellyn is treasurer. But the general membership—' Frobisher shrugged. 'It's probably best to let them think Harvey died by misadventure. It was well known he was a heavy drinker. Very likely, people will assume he had a heart attack.'

The MG turned onto the main drive. Soon, the clubhouse rose up before them. Constructed in Edwardian times, it was an imposing building with a porticoed entrance and tall windows that gave it a classical appearance. Electric lanterns lit up the frontage. By their light, de Silva saw that the entrance was flanked by flowerbeds in which a profusion of orange canna lilies licked like flames at the mellow stone walls. He was aware that the club's hallowed portals didn't welcome locals like himself; the membership was exclusively British. Deep down, de Silva had to admit that even though he had no desire to play golf, he wasn't entirely immune to feelings of resentment at being shunned in his own country. But it was his nature to adopt a philosophical attitude to things he could do nothing about. Tonight, in any case, he had more pressing matters to deal with.

CHAPTER 4

As they walked across the car park towards the portico, the front door opened, and Emerald Watson emerged. 'I've been watching out for you,' she said, reaching up to kiss David Hebden on the cheek. He squeezed her shoulder. 'Thank you, darling, but you really should have gone home. I thought you were going to ring Charlotte and ask her to send their driver to fetch you.'

'I wanted to be sure you were alright. And I've been perfectly safe here.' She smiled. 'I'm not entirely helpless you know.'

Her words didn't surprise de Silva. His impression of Emerald Watson was that she was a very down-to-earth young lady and not one likely to succumb to fits of the vapours. When she had decided to stay on in Nuala nearly two years ago, she had been a popular addition to the town's society, particularly where David Hebden was concerned. Their engagement had been announced quite recently. Until the marriage took place, however, she continued to lodge at the home of her friend, Charlotte Appleby.

'Anyway, I met Mark Brodie and he's been looking after me,' she went on. 'He bought me a whisky and soda, and we've been chatting.'

Something in Hebden's expression made de Silva suspect that the good doctor wasn't entirely happy with the thought that this man Mark Brodie had been entertaining his fiancée.

'Brodie's still up here, is he?' he asked with a frown. 'What about anyone else?'

'Just a few of the staff. Mark says the course being closed for the American ambassador's party this morning cast rather a dampener on the day from the members' point of view. And anyway, quite a few of them had already planned to go down to Hatton to watch the competition that was being held down there. Apart from you and me, only two other couples put themselves down to play up here this afternoon, and in the end, they decided it was too hot.'

Fortunate for them, reflected de Silva. They might have had the unpleasant experience of being the ones to find Bernard Harvey's body.

'Is Jasper in the car?' asked Emerald. 'Shall I take him for a walk? I think Mark would like a word with you.'

Hebden's brow furrowed. 'Well… I'm not sure—'

Emerald tapped his cheek with a slim finger. Her nails were painted fuchsia pink. 'I'll be perfectly fine. I promise not to go out of sight of the clubhouse.'

In the clubhouse lobby, a tall man with an athletic build greeted them. De Silva guessed he was in his mid-forties. He had blue-grey eyes and springy dark hair that he clearly didn't bother to tame with hair oil as did most of the male members of the British community.

'Good evening, gentlemen.' The voice was deep and gravelly.

'Evening, Brodie,' said Charlie Frobisher. Hebden merely grunted.

Mark Brodie turned to de Silva. 'We haven't met. I take it you're Inspector de Silva.'

'I am indeed, sir.'

'Emerald's told me a bit about this ghastly business. I'm glad Hebden managed to get hold of you. Not the way you intended to spend the start of your weekend, eh?'

'No, but police work is full of surprises.'

For a moment, Brodie looked at him thoughtfully, then gave a lopsided smile. 'I'm sure it is. Now, I didn't like to ask Emerald for too much detail for fear of distressing her, so I'd be grateful if you'd fill me in. Why don't we go to my office?'

The room he showed the three men into was spacious but rather gloomy. Panelled in dark wood, it was furnished with a partner's desk topped by red leather with a tooled gold border, several high-backed chairs, a large bookshelf containing box files and books, and several metal filing cabinets. Apart from a few papers on the desk, all the surfaces in the room were uncluttered. De Silva had the impression that Brodie was a man on top of his job.

Brodie took his place behind the desk and motioned them all to sit down. Reaching for a small silver box next to his desk lamp, he flipped open the lid and held it out. A rich aroma of expensive tobacco reached de Silva's nostrils. 'May I offer any of you gentlemen a cigarette?'

The three men shook their heads. There was a pause while Brodie took one himself and lit up then leant back in his chair. 'I understand you were the one to find the body, Hebden. Why don't you begin?'

'Emerald and I came across Bernard Harvey's body at about a quarter to four,' said David Hebden, a touch stiffly. 'I brought Emerald back to the clubhouse immediately and then telephoned the Residence. Archie Clutterbuck was tied up with the American ambassador and his party, so Frobisher agreed to come out and collect de Silva on his way.'

Brodie nodded. 'I was here with William Petrie and Archie Clutterbuck for the lunch with the American ambassador and his commercial attaché after their round of golf, but I wasn't included in the programme for the rest of the day. I must have been out looking for the head greenkeeper when you came to use the telephone. I needed to see him about a problem on the course. Something's been burrowing near the tenth green. I was concerned it might be pangolins after ants or termites. I don't want trouble like that getting out of hand.' He smiled. 'I like to run a tight ship.'

De Silva didn't doubt it. 'Were you able to find the greenkeeper, sir?' he asked, feeling it was time he contributed to the conversation. He made a mental note that he might need to speak to the greenkeeper at some point to corroborate Brodie's story.

Brodie turned to him. 'No, I decided to go back later to look for him again.' He gestured to the papers on his desk. 'I had work to do. Anyway, I was on the way back to my office when I spotted Emerald in the ladies' lounge.' He grinned at Hebden. 'Never leave a damsel in distress, eh?'

De Silva saw Hebden glower. He obviously didn't appreciate the implication that he had neglected his fiancée.

'What about the caddy?' asked Brodie. 'Any sign of him?'

'Not yet,' replied de Silva. 'I'll get my men onto it in the morning.'

'The sooner the better, I'd have thought. He needs to be found. If he's dead, he's no use to us, but if he's hiding, or wounded, it would put a different complexion on matters.' He paused and looked sharply at de Silva. 'I hasten to say, I'm not telling you how to do your job, Inspector.'

Brodie certainly gave a good imitation of someone who was, and callous into the bargain, but de Silva wasn't unused to interference. He'd always found it best to take it in his stride. 'Of course not, sir. But it's too late to start looking now.'

'He's worked at the club for many years,' Brodie went on, 'so I hesitate to accuse him, but might the motive be theft?'

'Unlikely,' said de Silva. 'A variety of expensive items

were still on the body.'

Brodie nodded. 'I take your point, although I wouldn't dismiss the possibility that this was a bungled robbery, perhaps, regrettably, with the caddy taking a part in it.'

'Do you know if he has a family?' asked de Silva. 'If so, I'll need to inform them that he's missing.'

'I have no idea, but the other caddies should be able to tell you. I suggest you speak to them.'

'Very good, sir. Can you tell us why Mr Harvey was playing when the course was closed to the general membership?'

'Yes, I can. Bernard Harvey considered himself to be entitled to special privileges up here at the club. I must admit, he's been very generous over the years. But he did like his largesse to be rewarded. He'd got into the habit of playing a few practice holes on his own every Friday morning. He said it suited his business commitments.'

Brodie grinned. 'I suspect he also liked a few holes on his own because, despite what he would have had you believe if he'd been here to speak for himself, he wasn't a particularly good golfer. In fact, it was a bit of a joke with some of the members that he spent more time waiting for his caddy to find his ball than hitting it. Harvey booked himself out to start at nine o'clock on the dot. His usual caddy was with him. The agreement was, however, that he would only play the back nine holes. I'd discussed it with the committee, and we decided that was the best way of diffusing an awkward situation. Even at his pace, Harvey should have been out of the way before Petrie, Clutterbuck and the Americans were ready to play those.'

He inhaled deeply and blew out a puff of smoke. 'Damned good job they didn't spot anything was amiss. Where exactly was the body found?'

'In the trees behind the rough at the sixteenth. It was actually my dog who found it,' interposed Hebden.

'I see.'

Brodie leant forward in his chair and stubbed the remains of his cigarette out in the green onyx ashtray on his desk. It was rather a fine one, decorated with a painted metal figure of a golfer in full swing. 'Beaten to it by a dog, eh, Inspector?' he said with a smile.

De Silva gave a polite smile in return. 'I'm afraid we shall have to deploy more than the skills of Doctor Hebden's dog, sir.'

Brodie's lips twitched. 'I imagine you will.'

'May I ask what your movements have been today?'

A slight look of irritation came over Brodie's face then vanished. 'Certainly, you may. I came up to the clubhouse just before half past eight this morning to be ready to welcome our guests. William Petrie was to partner Archie Clutterbuck, and the American ambassador was partnered by his commercial attaché. Once they'd set off on their round, I spent half an hour here in my office collecting together some papers. I was due to go to our treasurer, David Llewellyn's, house to do some work on the club accounts in advance of our upcoming Annual General Meeting. I stayed with Llewellyn until just after midday. After that, I drove back here, a journey of about ten minutes, in anticipation of the lunch party organised for the ambassador. The party broke up around half past three. After that, I came to my office for a short time to do some more paperwork, then went to look for the head greenkeeper as I explained earlier.'

'Does your work at the golf club take up all your time, sir?' asked de Silva.

'No, I'm the local agent for several of the tea exporting companies in Colombo. Fortunately, however, to all intents and purposes, I'm the master of my own time. It's up to me to decide how to use it. Today, with the function for the ambassador, and the AGM coming up, I decided to spend the day on golf club business.'

'Apart from yourself, were other committee members present at the lunch or at the club this morning?'

'David Llewellyn was at the lunch but didn't come up to welcome the ambassador before his round of golf. Archie Clutterbuck, who is our captain, was here all morning of course, and attended the lunch. The only other member of the committee is Tom Duncan.'

'Duncan's a prominent local solicitor,' interposed Hebden.

Brodie nodded. 'Regrettably, a business commitment prevented him from taking part in the occasion.' He glanced at his watch. 'I don't want to hurry you, gentlemen, but I have tomorrow to consider. I'd hate any of our members to have an unpleasant encounter during their round of golf. Is there anything that we need to do in respect of Bernard Harvey's body?'

'All dealt with,' said Frobisher. 'At least as far as it can be for the moment. As it was nearly dark, de Silva and I removed it to the old halfway hut and secured it there. I'm sure the inspector's search for the caddy tomorrow will be as discreet as possible and Hebden will also arrange for the undertakers to pick up Harvey's body tomorrow, won't you, Hebden?'

David Hebden nodded. 'Yes, and as I can do nothing more tonight, I think it's time I took Emerald home.'

'Of course,' said Brodie. 'I hope today's unpleasantness isn't going to put her off her golf. Such a charming lady would be greatly missed.'

'Good of you to say so,' said Hebden gruffly. His tone stirred de Silva's sympathy. Patently, Brodie's practised charm made the good doctor uncomfortable.

'By the way, how was Harvey killed?' asked Brodie, as the door closed behind Hebden. 'I didn't want to ask Emerald to go into detail.'

'A blow, or rather several of them, to the head,' said

Frobisher. 'Hebden believes the weapon would have been a golf club.'

Brodie grimaced. 'Nasty.'

Silence fell as the men contemplated Harvey's fate, then Brodie spoke again. 'Well, gentlemen, if there's nothing more I can do for you tonight, shall we leave it there? Before the evening gets much older, I take it you want to inform Mrs Harvey of her sad loss.'

Frobisher looked gloomy. Informing the relatives of a murder victim was always a task that de Silva too found extremely uncongenial.

'There's his grandson, Jack, as well,' Brodie continued. 'He lives at his grandfather's house. I expect you know him better than I do, Frobisher. You golf together sometimes, don't you? How do you think he'll take the news? I understand he and his grandfather didn't always see eye to eye.'

'So I believe. Jack told me on several occasions that his grandfather's standards were too exacting for comfort.'

'The age-old battle of the generations,' said Brodie ruefully. 'Nevertheless, I'm sure this will come as a blow to him.' He went to the door and held it open. 'If you need me tomorrow, Inspector, I intend to be here for most of the day. I'll see to it that the gate up at the halfway hut is locked first thing. We don't want any interference with the crime scene, do we? You'll have to collect the key from my office.'

Irritably, de Silva wished he had been the one to stipulate that the gate should be locked.

'And I'll see to it that Hebden and the undertakers are aware of it,' added Brodie.

De Silva thanked him and followed Frobisher out.

* * *

Left alone in his office, Mark Brodie went to the window and waited until they emerged onto the drive. He watched them as they got into the red MG and drove away. Returning to his desk chair, he sat deep in thought for several minutes, then rousing himself, he picked up the telephone and made the first of two calls. The first lasted only a few minutes, but the second, placed a few cigarettes later, took longer. When he had finished, Brodie pulled open a drawer in his desk, took out a torch and strode purposefully out of his office.

CHAPTER 5

'What do you know about Mr Harvey's grandson?' asked de Silva as the MG sped along, the brightness of its headlights creating a sharp contrast between the road and the dark walls of jungle on either side.

'Jack's father was Bernard Harvey's only child by his first wife. Jack was left an orphan when his parents died in a road accident. His grandfather brought him up, and now he works on the Harvey tea plantation.'

De Silva knew the place. It was one of the largest plantations in the area. He had often driven along the road that went past it and admired the splendid house one caught a glimpse of through the trees.

'I expect Harvey hoped Jack would take over the running of all his businesses in due course,' continued Frobisher. 'The trouble is, although Jack's a likeable fellow, he's lazy. He has some unsuitable friends too. They're – how shall I put it – far fonder of spending money than making it. Most of them are the sons of wealthy families up here in the Hill Country or in Kandy.'

A privileged world thought de Silva, and a dangerous one for a young man of weak character.

'Jack's told me several times that he has blazing rows with his grandfather over his activities.'

'What activities would they be?'

'Mainly his trips down to Colombo and Kandy. He

laughs about going on benders for days. When we played a round of golf a couple of weeks ago, he was full of stories about a club he visits in Kandy. The Blue Cat, I think it was called. As we were finishing our round, he made me promise not to mention the name when we went for a drink afterwards at the nineteenth hole. He didn't want his grandfather getting to hear about the place.' Frobisher grinned. 'Jack tried to get me to come along with him, but I said no, and he accused me of being an old sobersides.'

De Silva knew that a golf club bar was called the nineteenth hole, although he hadn't heard the expression "a bender" before. However, he got the general idea: Jack was of a very different stamp to Charlie Frobisher.

'For his own sake, I hope that Jack calms down now. The plantation has a very competent manager, a chap called Peter Hancock, but with Bernard Harvey dead, Jack will really need to learn how to take overall charge.'

'Are you certain that the business goes to Jack?' asked de Silva.

'That's what he's told me on several occasions. Apparently, Bernard Harvey's will leaves everything to him, but reserves a life interest to his stepmother, Elizabeth, enabling her to stay in the plantation house for as long as she wants. She's also entitled to be paid a very generous allowance. On occasion, I've heard Jack complain that she ought to be nicer to him, considering that one day, he would be the one who had so royally support her.'

'And do you have an opinion about the lady?'

'Elizabeth Harvey? I don't know a great deal about her, except that she's very glamorous and quite a lot younger than her husband was. I've only met her once, at one of the Residence's garden parties last year. I doubt she'll remember me.'

The road came out from the shelter of the trees, and the vast Harvey plantation lay before them, silvered by moonlight. The whereabouts of the plantation house was signalled by a blaze of lights. The size of the place made Sunnybank look like a cottage.

'Nearly there,' said Frobisher gloomily. 'I'm not looking forward to this. I suppose you've had to do it lots of times?'

'Sadly, quite a few, but it never gets any easier.'

They reached the bottom of the road leading up to the house. It was guarded by an imposing pair of wrought-iron gates, their tops bristling with arrow-shaped spikes. Frobisher sounded the MG's horn and a man emerged from the small hut on the far side. De Silva climbed out to speak to him and, reassured by the uniform de Silva had taken the precaution of donning before he left Sunnybank, the man soon opened the gates. A few moments later, they reached the gravel sweep in front of the house.

The first thing de Silva noticed was a magnificent cream and tan Rolls Royce Phantom that was parked there. Nearby, was a scarlet SSI Tourer.

Suppressing the desire to linger and admire the Rolls' elegant lines and supple cream leather and walnut interior, he turned his attention to the house. It was not much smaller than the clubhouse at the Royal Nuala Golf Club but far more modern in style. A loggia ran all the way across the façade, shielding the rooms beyond from view. A chocolate vine scrambled up the pillars supporting it and over its roof. De Silva smelt its delicious aroma of vanilla on the warm air. Huge brass or ceramic pots contained a profusion of orchids and succulent plants.

The magnificence of the mahogany front door, with its metal studs and massive door knocker in the shape of a snarling lion, was daunting. Shifting his weight from one foot to the other, de Silva was glad he had Frobisher to back him up.

Frobisher knocked, and the sound resonated inside the house. As it died away, footsteps approached. The servant who opened the door was smartly turned out in white turban, trousers and tunic embellished with gold frogging and crimson braid. He showed them into a spacious, marble-floored hall where they waited while he went to announce their arrival to Elizabeth Harvey.

'Beautiful place,' remarked Frobisher in an undertone. De Silva nodded; it certainly was. Intricate wood carvings and paintings of Oriental figures decorated the white walls. The doors to the rooms leading off the hall were also intricately carved with motifs of fruits, birds and flowers.

'Come this way, please,' said the servant when he returned. They followed him through a large drawing room furnished with antiques. As he passed the grand piano that stood near a pair of double doors leading to the garden, de Silva noticed many silver-framed photographs on top of it.

In the light of lanterns suspended from wrought-iron poles, Elizabeth Harvey lounged in a steamer chair on the verandah. She didn't get up, merely extending one hand in a languid gesture. The sleeve of her sea-green, chiffon dress hung from her arm like a waterfall.

'What a pleasure to see you again, Mr Frobisher. It was last summer at one of the Residence parties that we met, wasn't it?' A smile lit Elizabeth Harvey's immaculately made-up face. Her dark hair was cut short so that its artfully feathered ends curved to emphasise her delicate jawline. Long, sweeping lashes, and the kohl liner that rimmed her dark eyes, accentuated their lustre.

With a touch of amusement, de Silva noticed that Charlie Frobisher seemed to have lost his tongue. He was probably flattered to be remembered, and the lady's husky voice was very alluring. How contrived was it? It was hard to believe that she wasn't enjoying the effect she was having on the young man.

She turned her attention to de Silva, who braced himself, the unpleasant nature of the duty he was about to perform banishing the momentary lightening of his mood. Poor lady: they were about to give her news that would radically change her life.

A cough and the squeak of a leather-soled shoe distracted him. The young man who had been slouching against the verandah's balustrade straightened up. His eyes were bloodshot, and his clothes rumpled as if he had slept in them. He greeted Frobisher. 'Always a pleasure to see you, but why have you brought the old bill with you? I'm not aware I've robbed any banks lately.'

With an expression that bordered on boorishness, he looked de Silva up and down. Sensing that there was something underlying the young man's behaviour that had nothing to do with his presence, de Silva didn't rise to the bait.

Elizabeth Harvey raised an eyebrow. 'For goodness' sake, Jack! Are you going to carry on behaving like a bear with a sore head all evening? Inspector, please forgive my stepson. He and my husband argued last night, and—'

'Dammit, Elizabeth,' broke in Jack. 'Do you have to tell the whole world?' He drummed the fingers of one hand on the balustrade.

Elizabeth Harvey uncurled from her chair; she was tall for a woman, only a fraction shorter than de Silva's five foot ten inches, and the grace of her movements enhanced her willowy figure. She picked up a tall glass frosted with moisture. De Silva smelt gin and Angostura bitters. Going over to Jack, she touched his arm. 'Jack, dear, I'm sure everything will be alright. Your grandfather will get over it, but please, try not to provoke him again. Here – finish your drink. It'll be time for dinner soon.' She sighed. 'I think we'll have to give up waiting for Bernard. I gave him a lift to the golf club this morning, but he hasn't called for me to collect him yet. Knowing him, he'll have managed to get himself in on this lunch with the American ambassador, but he might at least have let me know if he was going to be out for dinner as well.'

Jack Harvey grunted. 'I suppose it's all my fault, and he's still angry with me.' He swung round to hunch over the balustrade.

Elizabeth Harvey let out a little snort of irritation. 'Do stop being childish. It's not a bad thing for either of you to have some time apart to simmer down. After you left last night, your grandfather was in no mood to talk, but when he gets back, just say you're sorry and do your best to make peace with him.'

She turned to Frobisher and de Silva. 'I'm sure you haven't come all this way to listen to family squabbles. Can I offer you any refreshment? Our butler makes an excellent gin sling.'

They both shook their heads, and she frowned. 'I hope this isn't something serious.'

Charlie Frobisher glanced uncomfortably at de Silva who took a deep breath before he spoke. 'I'm afraid we have bad news for you, ma'am. You might prefer to hear it inside.'

'Inside?' Elizabeth Harvey looked puzzled. 'No, whatever it is, you may as well tell us straight away.' She put a hand to her cheek, the other hand still holding Jack's spurned drink. 'Has something happened to my husband? Has he had an accident?'

'Not an accident, ma'am,' said Frobisher awkwardly.

Elizabeth Harvey's hand tightened on the glass. 'What on earth do you mean? Where is he? I want to see him.'

'I think it's better you don't, ma'am. It will only distress you.'

She stared at them, and de Silva saw comprehension dawn. As he had done on many previous occasions, he wished that there was some way of sparing a victim's family so much pain.

'You've come to tell me he's dead, haven't you?' asked Elizabeth Harvey. 'That's it, isn't it?'

'I'm very sorry, ma'am,' said de Silva. There was nothing for it now but to carry on. 'His body was found up at the golf course earlier this afternoon.'

Elizabeth Harvey swayed. There was a crash as the glass containing Jack's gin sling slipped from her grasp and smashed on the floor.

CHAPTER 6

'How dreadful,' said Jane sadly. 'What about his caddy? Surely, Harvey wouldn't have carried his own clubs?'

'Naturally not. According to Mark Brodie, the club secretary, he was Harvey's regular man and has been at the club for many years. There was no evidence of theft, so I doubt he attacked Harvey, although Mark Brodie maintains we shouldn't rule out a bungled robbery to which he might have been party.'

'He may have been killed too, or perhaps he's lying injured somewhere.'

'Perhaps. We've not found him so far, but I'll get Prasanna and Nadar onto that in the morning. I'm afraid that if he was injured, he may not survive a night in the jungle.'

'Oh dear, it's terrible to think of what he would have suffered – what he might still be suffering. Must the search really wait until tomorrow?'

'I fear so, my love. It would be hopeless looking for him in the dark.' He didn't like to distress Jane even more, but privately, he doubted the search would produce a happy result anyway. 'I don't know yet whether he had a family. Brodie couldn't enlighten me and suggested I ask the other caddies. Prasanna and Nadar can talk to them when they go up to the club to search.'

'Poor Mrs Harvey, she's very young to lose her husband, and in such tragic circumstances.'

'You've met her?'

'Once or twice, although she's not part of any of the usual Nuala sets – the bridge club, the tennis club, Florence's sewing circle – that kind of thing. I've never seen her at church either. I suppose she likes to keep herself to herself.' She frowned. 'Oh dear, perhaps we should have made more effort to include her, and we must now; if she welcomes company, that is.'

'You have a kind heart, my love, but you may find you are rebuffed. I expect Mrs Harvey would have joined in with Nuala's activities if she had wanted to.'

'I suppose so. Most people do.' She rubbed her cheek with a forefinger. 'Although one ought at least to try. It is a little awkward as I hardly know her, but she shouldn't be alone at a time like this.'

'Don't worry, she won't be. Her stepson, Jack Harvey, was there when Frobisher and I went to the house.' He sighed. 'It's never easy. How does anyone break the news gently in situations like these? Frobisher admitted to me it wasn't the kind of a thing he'd had to deal with before, and he managed very well, but I'm afraid Mrs Harvey collapsed and there was quite a to-do.'

'Hardly surprising. How did the stepson take the news?'

'He was already in a bad mood when we arrived. He'd had a row with his grandfather the previous evening. He told Frobisher and me that he'd driven off to Kandy and spent the night down there, so sadly, he never had the opportunity to make his peace with him.'

'What was he doing in Kandy?'

'He claims he spent the evening at a club that he frequents. It's called the Blue Cat. He didn't leave there until this morning. From the look of him, I imagine he didn't get much sleep. He said he'd stopped on the way at a roadhouse to buy petrol and something to eat and didn't get back to Nuala until around five o'clock.'

'Did Mrs Harvey recover sufficiently to bear his story out?'

'Yes. And even when it would have been understandable if the bad news and her subsequent indisposition sent everything else out of her mind, she seemed very concerned to comfort him and reassure him that if circumstances had been different, he would have been able to repair the damage done with his grandfather. From what I've heard though, that might be over-optimistic. This was, apparently, only one incident of many. The relationship between them was a difficult one. Charlie Frobisher told me that Jack's a pleasant fellow but lazy and rather wild. He has unsuitable friends. Most of them the sons of wealthy families up here in the Hill Country or down in Kandy. Frobisher plays golf with him occasionally, but he doesn't socialise with him otherwise.'

'I don't expect he does. I gather Charlie Frobisher's far happier trekking in the jungle or climbing mountains than drinking in clubs. Florence tells me that he's a very diligent young man where his work is concerned. She thinks he'll go far. In fact, he's rather a favourite of hers. She even trusts him to walk Angel if she's called away for any reason.'

De Silva grinned. 'That *is* an honour.' With amusement, he pictured the tall, rangy young man in charge of the little household mop of a dog that was like a beloved child to Archie Clutterbuck's wife, Florence. 'In any event, Jack's way of life caused a lot of trouble between him and his grandfather, who wanted someone hard-working and ambitious to follow in his footsteps.'

'I'm surprised that Elizabeth Harvey wasn't more concerned about her husband being absent all day if he'd only gone out for a morning round of golf.'

'She knew about the American ambassador's visit. Apparently, Bernard Harvey had been very pleased with himself that he'd managed to play some of his usual round, overriding the morning's arrangements for the course to be closed to members. She assumed that he'd managed to wiggle himself an invitation to the lunch and then spent the rest of the afternoon at the club.'

'Wangle, dear,' said Jane absent-mindedly. 'All the same, it sounds an odd marriage if she's used to him not telling her what he's doing.'

'Maybe not used to it. Don't forget, there was the argument with his grandson, Jack. Harvey might still have been in a bad mood and that made him uncommunicative.'

'That's true. I suppose in the circumstances, one shouldn't read too much into it. But why would Harvey be given special treatment for his round of golf?'

'I understand from Mark Brodie, the club secretary, with whom Frobisher and I had a few words when we came back to the clubhouse after Harvey's body had been found, that he gave a lot of money to the club over the years. He kicked up a fuss if his generosity wasn't rewarded in the form of special privileges.'

'Did you find out what Elizabeth Harvey was doing during the day?'

'She said she'd driven her husband to the golf club at around 8.30 this morning then had gone on to an appointment at a clinic in Hatton called the Victoria.'

'I've heard of it. It's very exclusive. I wonder why she had an appointment there.'

'I didn't like to ask at such a time.'

'That's understandable.'

'Afterwards, she had a lunch date at the Crown Hotel. She assumed her husband would call the Crown to say he was ready to be picked up but had seen no particular cause for alarm when this didn't happen. She thought he'd decided to keep out of the house for a while, so she simply drove herself home.'

He smiled. 'The car is magnificent – a Rolls Royce

Phantom. At any other time, I would have loved the chance to take a better look at it.'

'She must be a good driver to manage such a large car.'

'I imagine she is. She returned home shortly before three o'clock. Hopefully, it won't be too hard to verify all of that. Once she was at home, we only have the word of her servants to rely on, but Hebden's opinion was that Harvey was killed in the morning.'

'But until then, we have to look on her as a suspect.'

'At this stage, I can't rule anyone out, even though she seems an unlikely murderer. Whoever attacked Bernard Harvey must have been strong as well as ruthless. I'll need to confirm Jack's alibi too.'

Going to Kandy himself would take up the best part of a day, and he would rather not spend that much time. But the club was unlikely to have a telephone; they were rarely found outside government offices and the upper echelons of the British community. In any case, a visit was usually best. 'I haven't decided yet,' he went on, 'but I may telephone the police station at Kandy and ask if someone would go around to the Blue Cat and make inquiries for me.'

'Have you had a chance to speak to Archie Clutterbuck about what's happened yet?'

De Silva shook his head. 'But I hope Charlie Frobisher will have done. He offered to take on the job, but he'll have to wait until Archie finishes today's engagements with the American ambassador and his party. William Petrie was up in Nuala too but had to go back to Kandy, leaving Archie as the main host for the Americans. It sounds like it's a big event. No doubt the last thing Archie would want is for it to be interrupted by a murder.'

'I expect you're right.'

In truth, he was glad to have some time without his boss breathing down his neck and interfering. Admirable as Archie was, he was always keen to wrap up a problem as quickly as possible and do things his own way. De Silva pictured him: gruff and gimlet-eyed. He could be perfectly affable, but when he wanted something done, and done quickly, he was the epitome of the British bulldog.

'Is there anything left for dinner? Lunch seems a long time ago.'

Jane went to the drawing room door and put her hand on the bell pull. 'I wasn't sure what time you'd come home, so I told the cook to keep everything hot. I'll tell him to serve up as soon as he can.'

'Excellent. I'll go and wash my hands.'

* * *

'I feel better already,' said de Silva, surveying the dishes on the dining table: a large bowl of rice, fragrant with turmeric; his favourite cashew and pea curry; a stack of roti bread, baked to a puffy golden brown; green jackfruit curry, and a dish of brinjal relish. He spooned a mound of rice onto his plate and added portions of the curries, ending with a generous helping of the spicy aubergine pickle.

'Have you decided who your main suspects are yet?' asked Jane, tearing some roti into neat pieces.

De Silva raised his spoon from his plate and waved it to indicate that his mouth was too full to speak. 'The committee members have to be high on the list,' he said when he had swallowed his food. 'They all knew that Harvey was up at the course that morning, but the club secretary, Mark Brodie, made it clear he'd otherwise kept the matter quiet as he didn't want the general run of members to feel aggrieved that Harvey had been given preferential treatment. Even though it did turn out to be extremely unfortunate for him that he was,' he added.

'So, if anyone else knew that Harvey was going to be

42

playing, he must have told them himself, or it was by chance that they found it out.'

'Yes. I only saw Brodie, but Charlie Frobisher filled me in on the others as he was driving me back here. The treasurer is a man called David Llewellyn. He's an accountant, so he was an ideal choice for the job. He's in his fifties: a bit of a grey man. Unmarried. People have no objection to him, but he has no close friends. The nearest seems to be Brodie, but Frobisher thinks that's just because the business of the golf club throws them together. Apparently, he never got on well with Bernard Harvey.'

'Why was that?'

'Frobisher wasn't sure, but he's heard rumours that in the past, some of Llewellyn's clients were put out of business by Harvey. If it's true, Llewellyn might have resented Harvey for being the cause of his losing money.'

'Did he have much to do with Harvey at the club?'

'Frobisher never saw them playing together or drinking in the bar. He believed the only time they spoke was if Harvey stood up to query the accounts at the golf club's AGMs, as apparently, he did on several occasions. According to Frobisher, Harvey liked to throw his weight around to make the point that he was a big-shot businessman. I understand the issues he raised were rarely important; more like flea-picking.'

Jane smiled. 'Nit-picking, dear.'

'Ah.'

He wiped up the last of his pea and cashew curry with a piece of roti. 'Mark Brodie told me he and Llewellyn spent the main part of the morning going over the accounts for a club meeting. He, Brodie, that is, had been up at the club early to welcome Archie, William Petrie, and the Americans before they started their round of golf. Both he and Llewellyn returned to the club for the lunch that had been arranged.'

'What did you think of Mark Brodie?'

'Very sure of himself. I suppose you'd call him handsome. He was turning on the charm with Emerald Watson.'

'I don't expect Doctor Hebden liked that.'

'No. Anyway, Brodie seemed unruffled by events. I suppose if he wasn't close to Harvey, there's no reason why he would be distressed, but my impression was that he's a man who takes most things in his stride. All the same, I'll need to verify his story.'

'And if it's true, that would rule out Mr Llewellyn as well,' mused Jane. 'Does that leave us with anyone else who's on the committee?'

'There's Archie; he's the captain, then lastly, a man called Tom Duncan, who's the vice-captain. He's a solicitor.'

'Oh yes, I know his wife. Her name's Ella. A rather quiet lady. She comes to events sometimes. It's hard to find a topic of conversation that draws her out, although Florence told me she's fond of poetry, so perhaps I should try that. The last time I saw her was at that bring-and-buy sale last month to raise funds for the church. I wondered if she'd been unwell. She's usually very smartly dressed, with her hair and make-up just so, but that day she was very pale, and her dress didn't fit well, as if she'd lost weight. When I asked her how she was, she said something about a stomach upset, and I noticed she left early. What did Charlie Frobisher have to say about her husband?'

'That he's rather dry with a remote manner, but he's well respected. Frobisher thinks he handles more commercial and private work than criminal cases. I don't believe I've come across him. According to Frobisher, Bernard Harvey was one of his clients.'

He reached for a piece of roti. 'According to Brodie, Duncan had business commitments that prevented him from coming up to the club to attend the occasion. So, around the time when Hebden thinks Harvey was murdered, only the staff were up at the clubhouse to prepare the lunch. I doubt any of them had time to walk to the far side of the course.'

'Anyway, why would any of them want to kill Bernard Harvey?'

'I can't answer that. I do know that there's a gate that gives access to the course very close to the place where Harvey was found. It hasn't been kept locked, but Brodie's seeing to it that it will be from now on.'

'But if someone who isn't on the committee killed Harvey, how did they know when and where to find him?'

'The first person who springs to mind is Jack Harvey. For the present, we only have his word for it that he wasn't in Nuala at the relevant time. As to how he would have known where and when to waylay his grandfather, if Harvey's wife knew he was playing golf that morning, presumably Jack did too. He's a golfer, so no doubt he could estimate how long his grandfather would need to reach the place where he was killed.'

'What a terrible thought. I hope it's not true.'

De Silva shrugged. 'Charlie Frobisher's account of Jack inclines me to think the young man's no more a killer than his stepmother, but I can't rule anything out yet.'

'Did Charlie have any helpful suggestions to offer about who might have wanted Bernard Harvey dead?'

'I understand he wasn't a popular man at the club, but that's hardly a motive for murder.'

'What about outside the club?'

'The field is wide open. Don't forget that gate isn't kept locked. Anyone who knew where it was could have used it to get onto the course. I hope I don't end up needing to question half the town,' he added gloomily.

Jane frowned. 'What if it's someone who has a grudge against the club, or even the British generally?'

It was undeniable that it was a possibility that had

already occurred to him. There was a great deal of unrest and opposition to British rule in India, although there had been no serious incidents of it spreading to Ceylon – yet. But it was all the more reason to find the killer quickly. What if they struck again?

For a while, they ate in silence, the disturbing thought hanging unspoken between them.

'Would you like anything to follow?' asked Jane when the main course was over. 'Cook bought some nice ripe mangoes in the market this morning.'

He sighed. 'My appetite seems to have deserted me. Will they keep for breakfast?'

Jane looked at him sympathetically. 'Try not to brood, dear. I'm sorry now that I spoke.'

He shrugged. 'Don't be sorry. The same thought had already occurred to me.'

They moved out onto the verandah. The cushion in his favourite chair expelled a little whump of air as de Silva settled into it and looked up at the stars. The night sky always soothed him; the thought that the stars had glittered up there for billions of years, and would probably go on for billions more, had a way of putting life in perspective. Funny to think that when they'd sat on the verandah yesterday after dinner, he'd had nothing more important to do than watch the stars and try to remember their names. Usually, he soon left that to Jane and just enjoyed admiring them. She was much better at reading the night sky than he was.

There was a soft footfall, and one of the servants appeared carrying a tray of tea. Jane let the pot brew for a little while then poured out for them both and handed him a cup. Scented steam rose to his nostrils; the delicate, pale liquor smelt of pine and honey. 'Ah, white tea,' he said. 'What a treat.'

Jane smiled. 'I thought you deserved one tonight.'

'You're very good to me.'

When he had finished the first cup, she gestured to the pot. 'Would you like another?'

He nodded. Sipping his second cup more slowly, he considered where to start in the morning. The first job, he decided, must be to go to the police station and organise Prasanna and Nadar to search for the caddy. They were on duty in the morning on Saturdays.

Then he wanted to pay another visit to the secretary of the golf club, Mark Brodie, and talk to David Llewellyn and Tom Duncan. The telephone call to the police at Kandy about Jack Harvey's story might have to wait until Monday. He had better deal with Kandy himself. At this stage, he'd prefer not to get embroiled in a lot of paperwork that might prove unnecessary. He still had a few former colleagues working in Kandy. Hopefully, they would be amenable to making enquiries at the Blue Cat for him. He ought to look into Elizabeth Harvey's alibi at some stage, even though he didn't seriously anticipate that he would find anything amiss.

'Penny for your thoughts, dear?'

Jane's voice brought him back to the present. 'Oh, I was just thinking about what needs to be done. It is unfortunate tomorrow is a Saturday, but I hope to be able to make some progress.'

'Well, I think what you need now is a good night's sleep.'

He looked at his watch; it was nearly midnight. 'You're right as usual. Time for bed.'

CHAPTER 7

The soothing properties of white tea worked their magic. He slept soundly until he was woken by Jane. Too soundly. He had planned to start his day earlier. There was a lot to do.

First, he telephoned the station and, finding Prasanna and Nadar already there, gave them their instructions. They would have to use their bicycles to get up to the golf club. Afterwards, he washed and dressed, then fortified by a good breakfast of string hoppers, sambol, dhal, and egg curry, he kissed Jane goodbye and picked up his keys from the table in the hall. 'I won't be back for lunch. If there's time after I've spoken to the committee members available, I'll join Prasanna and Nadar on the search for the caddy.'

'Good luck, dear. If you find him alive, I do hope he's not too badly injured.'

* * *

The drive up to the golf club gave him time to think. As he motored along the sun dappled lanes, he went over the previous evening's encounter with Elizabeth Harvey and her stepson. Could Jack be the guilty party? That he stood to benefit from his grandfather's death made it an obvious deduction, but would he want the responsibility that great riches entailed? Wasn't it easier to be the pampered grandson of a rich man, even if, from time to time, he was obliged to endure the rough side of his grandfather's tongue? It was possible that Jack deluded himself, he supposed. But what about the violence of the attack? Was Jack really the kind of young man who would have the stomach for such a horrific assault?

His thoughts turned to Elizabeth Harvey. After the initial shock, she had taken the news with dignity, and that was to her credit. But there was something about her behaviour that raised a scintilla of doubt in de Silva's mind. Was Jane's first instinct the right one? Should Elizabeth have been more concerned that Harvey hadn't contacted the Crown for her to pick him up from the golf club? Even if she was used to her husband and her stepson arguing, what about her remarks to him? Yes, it was generous of her to try to comfort Jack when she had every reason to forget the feelings of another, yet she had not only tried to comfort him, she had mentioned several times that he hadn't returned from Kandy until five o'clock.

De Silva had two issues with that. Firstly, how could she be sure? She only had Jack's word for it that he'd come straight to the plantation house, and a woman who seemed as intelligent as she did could be expected to think of that. Secondly, why had she mentioned the time more than once? Was she hoping that repetition would make Jack's story convincing? He made a mental note to take that further.

The Morris drew to a halt in front of the clubhouse. There were already more than a dozen cars in the driveway, and it was busy with golfers arriving and caddies carrying their bags. He parked the Morris in the shade of a clump of palm trees and walked over to the entrance.

He felt more conspicuous than he had done the previous evening. Men he passed, presumably members, cast him unfriendly looks. When Prasanna and Nadar came to collect the key to the gate, they had probably felt at even more of a disadvantage. He squared his shoulders and lifted his chin. He wouldn't be intimidated, despite the fact that the aim of the Royal Nuala Golf Club appeared to be to make non-members feel unwelcome. In the lobby, he gave his name and asked for Mark Brodie; he only had to wait a few moments before Brodie came out to greet him.

'And what can I do for you this morning, Inspector?' asked Brodie when they were ensconced in his office. With the morning sun streaming through the mullioned windows, making the panelled walls glow, it looked less gloomy that it had done the previous evening.

'I'd like to establish how easy it would be for someone to get to the place on the course where Mr Harvey's body was found. I understand there's a perimeter fence. Can you tell me whether it is in good repair?'

'To the best of my knowledge, it is, but I don't usually inspect it myself. I leave that up to the head greenkeeper. I believe he's assiduous in his duties. It's advisable to keep elephants out.'

'You mentioned pangolins last night.'

'Ah yes. I suppose small animals burrow underneath or find their way through holes low down in the fence. It's virtually impossible to prevent all incursions. As to whether a man could fit through them, I wouldn't like to say.'

'So, would you say that the gate near the halfway hut is the most likely way in?'

'I imagine it is.'

'Do many people know it's there?'

Brodie shrugged. 'The ground staff if they've come across it while maintaining the fence. Otherwise, I can't give you a definite number. Now that the halfway hut is disused, there's no reason for members or delivery men to go there.'

'But would any of the members know it was there?'

'Possibly. Some were probably here when it was still in

use, and they might have mentioned it to members joining since then, but it was before my time. I came up here about six years ago. Before that, I was in Colombo for a few years.'

'Where were you previously?'

'India. Up north in the tea country.' He took a cigarette from the silver box on his desk, lit it and inhaled. 'How are your men getting on with searching the area for Harvey's caddy? I pointed them in the right direction when they came here earlier on to pick up the key to the gate.'

'I've had no news, but I'll be joining them up there later. I hope it won't be long before we find him.'

'Likewise.'

'Can you think of anyone at all who might have wanted Harvey dead?'

Brodie pondered then shook his head. 'No, I can't, Inspector. He wasn't popular at the club, but as far as I know, he had no serious enemies among the membership. Outside the club, I rarely met him socially. I can't tell you much about what his relationships were with his business associates.'

'But you do know something?'

'Tom Duncan, our vice-captain, did a considerable amount of legal work for him. Duncan intimated on a few occasions that Harvey was a difficult client. Despite that, the amount of work he gave Duncan's firm made it worthwhile putting up with his, shall we say, foibles. I doubt Harvey would have wanted to fall out irredeemably with Tom Duncan either. As the saying goes, Duncan knew where the bodies were buried.' He stubbed out his cigarette. 'My apologies; that remark was in bad taste. I take it Harvey's wife has been informed?'

'She has, and Harvey's grandson.'

Brodie rolled his eyes. 'Not a young man to step confidently into the breach, I'm afraid. And from the little I've heard of the widow, she doesn't know one end of a tea bush or an account ledger from the other, nor would she care to find out. I expect she hopes to be kept in luxury, as in her husband's day, with no effort on her part. From what I've heard, the poor sap worshipped her.' He paused. 'At some stage, I suppose I should send condolences on behalf of the club. Harvey was, after all, a long-standing member.'

Suppressing the thought that Brodie's reaction was less than gallant, de Silva reflected, as he had done on many other occasions, that he was lucky to have Jane as his wife.

'You mentioned yesterday evening that Harvey and his grandson didn't always get on well. Can you tell me more about that?'

'Oh, Harvey liked to shoot his mouth off, and his touch paper was easily lit. More than once, I heard him in the bar threatening to disinherit the lad, but I doubt he was serious.' He raised an eyebrow. 'Jack was incautious enough to josh him about his golf, probably in retaliation when Harvey criticised him for neglecting to do something at the plantation. Jack was a far better player than his grandfather would ever be. I believe that rankled at times, although Harvey was obviously fond of Jack. I imagine the lad will rely heavily on Peter Hancock now.'

'The manager at the plantation?'

'Yes.'

'Do you know much about him?'

'Very little. He's a taciturn chap. Not a golfer, but he plays a useful game of cricket. Played for the Nuala First XI once or twice.' Brodie half rose from his chair. 'Are there any other members you'd like to speak to, Inspector?'

'The remaining members of the committee, if that's possible.'

'I've seen David Llewellyn about the place this morning and informed him of what's happened. I'll find out for you if he's still here. The committee room's free if you'd like to meet him there.'

The committee room was panelled in the same dark wood as Mark Brodie's office but considerably larger. A massive mahogany table surrounded by twelve chairs took up the centre of the room. Plum velvet drapes curtained the windows and at one end of the room, there was a stone fireplace decorated with armorial shields that would have looked more at home in a baronial hall. Tall bay windows with mullioned panes, some of them inset with yellow, blue, and red stained glass, offered a view over the clubhouse terrace and the fairways beyond. A sign directed golfers to the first tee. Coming in from the left was a broad footpath that de Silva assumed led to and from the club's locker rooms.

As he waited for David Llewellyn, de Silva studied the large portrait above the stone fireplace. It was of King George VI when he was still Duke of York – a similar likeness hung in the drawing room at the Residence. George had become king after his elder brother, Edward, had abdicated, following a reign of less than a year. The urgent need to remove portraits of Edward and put ones of George in their place in government buildings all over the Empire must have given British civil servants quite a headache. What had happened to the unwanted pictures of the former king? Had they been destroyed? Painted over? Consigned ignominiously to dusty lumber rooms? Or did they remain on show somewhere – a reminder of the power, or folly, depending on one's point of view, of love? Poor George, he didn't have his brother's good looks and glamour. His troubled eyes peered out from a face with rather plain features. People said he was afflicted by a terrible stammer.

The door handle clicked, and David Llewellyn came in; another man who looked uncomfortable in his own skin. De Silva guessed he was in his mid-fifties. With his shaggy grey hair, stooped bearing, and lugubrious air, he reminded de Silva of a night heron.

'Good afternoon, Inspector. I don't see how I'm going to be able to help you much,' he said apologetically, 'but Brodie told me you'd like a word.' His voice had a lilt that de Silva didn't recognise.

Llewellyn went to stand by the fireplace. Its confident grandeur made him look even more downtrodden than before.

'In any case, thank you for sparing your time, sir.'

'Dreadful business. Harvey wasn't well liked but that's hardly the point.'

'Did you know him well?'

The night heron ruffled his feathers and shifted his weight. 'Not well.' He scowled. 'I won't waste your time with pretence, Inspector. Ask virtually anyone, and they'll tell you we had a mutual dislike that he made less effort to conceal than, I hope, did I. I've been a loyal servant of this club for twenty years. Bernard Harvey had no respect for loyalty.'

De Silva considered asking him to expand on his remarks, but seeing the pain in Llewellyn's eyes, he refrained. Knowing the British character, he doubted the man would open up much anyway, particularly to a stranger. He would stick to the usual line of questioning.

'As a formality, may I ask what your movements were yesterday morning?'

'I thought Brodie would have already told you about the business we were engaged in.'

'If you don't mind, sir, I'd like to hear it from you as well.' De Silva took out his notebook.

Llewellyn looked irritable. 'If you insist.' He cleared his throat. 'I breakfasted at home. My house servants will vouch for that if you ask them. Brodie arrived shortly before half past nine, by which time I had read the newspaper.

Of course, it was full of talk about the American ambassador's visit and photographs of him being received at the Residence.'

De Silva recalled Jane reporting that Florence had been in quite a fluster about that.

'Roosevelt, the American president, has been keen for some time to promote Anglo-American trade,' Llewellyn went on. 'He sees trade as the best way of protecting world peace in these uncertain times. Ceylon must do her bit. But I digress – Brodie and I spent several hours in my study, where we looked over accounts and prepared the paperwork for next month's AGM. At midday, Brodie drove back to the club and I followed. Clutterbuck, William Petrie, and the ambassador and his commercial attaché were just finishing their round. We had drinks in the bar then went into luncheon.'

He raised an eyebrow. 'If it's any help to you, Inspector, we were served beef consommé, lamb chop, and Bakewell tart. Afterwards, I returned home. As far as I'm aware, Brodie planned to stay up at the club. He had other business to see to.'

De Silva rested his pencil on the open page of his notebook. 'Thank you, sir. You've been very helpful. Finally, is there anything at all you can think of that might help the investigation?'

The night heron tucked his chin into his chest and was silent. At last, he looked up. 'Nothing comes to mind, Inspector. I'm sorry I can't be more use to you.'

CHAPTER 8

As de Silva reached the entrance lobby, the door to Mark Brodie's office opened and Brodie emerged. 'Will you come in for a moment, Inspector?'

De Silva thanked him and followed him into the office. Brodie closed the door and sat down but didn't offer de Silva a seat.

'I hope the interview was satisfactory. Llewellyn's a gloomy bugger but a good man for all that. Did he have much to tell you?'

'With respect, sir, it would be most improper of me to divulge that.'

Brodie's brow furrowed. He picked up a glass paper-weight and weighed it in his palm, clearly irritated. 'I take your point,' he said grudgingly after a moment. 'Anything else I can do for you?'

'I'd like to talk to the other member of your committee, Mr Duncan. Where can I find him?'

'He's unlikely to be at the club. He isn't playing today. Telephoned to cancel his game early this morning – trouble with a bad back, apparently. It flares up from time to time. I can call him for you, if you wish. I expect he's at home.'

'Thank you. Is he aware of what's happened?'

'I spoke to him briefly last night, I thought that as a member of the committee, he should be told Harvey had been found dead, but I was unable to give him a great deal more information.'

Pulling a leather-bound book towards him, Brodie opened it and found the number, then swivelled the book for de Silva to see the address. While the telephone rang, de Silva jotted it down in his notebook. It sounded as if a servant had answered, and there was a long pause while Brodie waited for Duncan to come on the line.

'Duncan! Mark Brodie here.' Brodie's tone was brisk. 'About this business of Bernard Harvey. I have the police here.' He paused to listen to what Duncan was saying at the other end of the line before continuing. 'No developments yet, but the chap with me now will fill you in in more detail, I expect. He wants to come up and see you when it's convenient. His name? Inspector—' He threw a questioning look at de Silva who said his name. A point to Mark Brodie, he thought wryly. He was sure the secretary hadn't really forgotten.

'Inspector de Silva... yes... good... I'll tell him.'

He put down the receiver. 'He'll spare you half an hour tomorrow after he and his wife return from church. Will twelve o'clock do for you?'

The question was obviously rhetorical.

'Thank you. I'll go up to the halfway hut now and see how my men are getting on.'

'You do that. You'll find Frobisher with them. He was here when they arrived to collect the key to the gate this morning and offered to lend a hand. The undertakers have already removed Harvey's body, by the way.'

De Silva thanked him and took his leave. Outside, he closed his eyes and took a deep breath. A rather scratchy meeting, but there was no harm in knowing who one was up against. In Brodie's defence, he did have the reputation of the club to protect, and his attitude wasn't uncommon among the British community.

* * *

As he drove to the halfway hut, he thought about what Llewellyn had said about trade with the Americans and troubled times. It brought back a conversation he'd had months ago with William Petrie on the way to Egypt on *The Jewel of the East*. It was impossible to be unaware that in some circles, the rise to power in Germany of this man Hitler was causing concern in Europe, and further afield. Some people even said there might be another war. If there was, where would Ceylon stand? She was little more than a grain of sand under the British lion's huge paw, but she might be called upon to do her bit, as she had been in the Great War. Would a call to arms provide a catalyst for change? With the unrest in India, might his own country-men start to question why they should fight for the British or tolerate being ruled by them for much longer?

The gate was open when he arrived at the entrance. Carefully negotiating the rutted track that led to the half-way hut, he brought the Morris to a halt on the patch of cleared ground beside it and climbed out of the car. There was no sign of Frobisher, Prasanna, or Nadar. He might spend a long time searching for them. He reached through the Morris's window on the driver's side and honked the horn several times. A few minutes elapsed before Charlie Frobisher emerged from the trees. He looked very hot and dusty.

'Good afternoon, Inspector. We've found Harvey's golf clubs now. Turns out they weren't far from the course. My guess is whoever killed him only moved them a short way off, not wanting to attract attention too soon after Harvey was killed. Otherwise, I'm afraid I don't have much to report. We decided to divide the area up as it's more extensive than you may think. Your men have gone that way.' He pointed to the east. 'I've been looking in the opposite direction.'

'It's very good of you to lend a hand.'

'Not at all. The boss asked me to if I had any time to spare. Unfortunately, I'm beginning to doubt whether this caddy will still be alive if we find him, but we ought to do our best.'

A sentiment Jane would approve of.

'Did my men manage to find out anything about him?'

'The other caddies they spoke to were sure he has no family.'

In the circumstances, that was a blessing. 'Well, let's not give up hope yet.' De Silva looked to the north. 'Shall I take that direction?'

'By all means. We agreed that if any of us saw something, we would whistle, then come back here and wait for the others to arrive.'

De Silva fetched a flask of water and the stout stick he had brought with him from the Morris and set off. As he walked, he beat a path in front of him, alert for the flicker of a sinuous tail or the flash of a scaly pattern that would announce there was a snake nearby. He also scanned low branches for the tell-tale arabesque of a basking reptile. More than once, he felt a frisson of anxiety, but only lianas and coils of moss, wispy and grey as an old man's beard, hung from the trees.

Soon, concentration on the task in hand calmed him. As he always did when he went into the jungle, he felt as if he had been sucked into the heart of a huge, vibrating engine. In the close air, so humid that he saw beads of moisture gleaming on every leaf and petal, he sensed everything growing. Trees, flowers, mosses, and lichen, living out the mystery of their secret lives. Lords of it all were the trees. For hundreds of years, they had stood here, shading the plants in the understory; the detritus they sloughed off forming a carpet of decay that filled the air with a pungent, sickly odour. It was strange to think that not so far away, this primaeval world had been tamed to provide fairways and greens covered with nothing but clipped grass.

After ten minutes, he thought he'd found what he was looking for. It was a place where branches looked to have been recently piled up against the trunk of a towering rubber tree. He took a gulp of water from his flask and set to work moving them. Soon, his hands were scratched from the rough bark, and at intervals, he stopped to swat away the small colonies of insects he disturbed.

Suddenly, he realised they were velvet ants, and stepped back. Their sting was an experience he had no desire to repeat. There might be poisonous scorpions too.

He'd moved enough branches for there to be wide gaps between the ones that remained. Using his stick, he poked at the earth between. Under the carpet of leaves, it was solid. After all, it was unlikely he would find the caddy's body there. Straightening up, he arched his back and massaged it with his fingers. Then for the third time, he mopped his face with his handkerchief. Hopefully, Frobisher, Prasanna and Nadar were having better luck than he was.

Then he froze.

Close to his left foot, something was making a rustling sound in the leaves. A snake? He fought back the urge to run, but the tiny snout that poked out belonged to a jungle shrew. It regarded him with bright, wary eyes then scuttled away. De Silva glanced at the sun, cradled high up in the tree canopy. Already, it was starting its descent. Enough of this; he hadn't eaten for hours and he suspected the others hadn't either.

* * *

'I take it from your expressions that you've had no luck,' said Mark Brodie, meeting them as they walked into the lobby.

Frobisher shrugged. 'I'm afraid not. We'll have to go out again if there's time before dark, but we need to eat. Can the kitchen rustle up something for us?'

'I'll see what can be done. Take a seat in the committee room while you're waiting. I'll have some cold drinks brought to you. You must be parched.'

'I certainly am, and I expect these gentlemen are too, but I'd like to go and wash first.' Frobisher held up his hands; the palms were stained green and the nails rimmed with dirt. De Silva noticed his own were no better.

In the committee room, Prasanna and Nadar stood irresolutely by the door. Frobisher pulled out a couple of chairs from under the long, mahogany table. 'Take the weight off your feet, for goodness' sake. You've worked hard.'

'Thank you, sir,' said Prasanna, sitting down. Nadar followed with an audible sigh of relief. De Silva's bones creaked as he sank into another chair. The room smelt of lavender-scented polish and old leather. Altogether more pleasant than the odour of death and decay that had been in his nostrils in the jungle.

To de Silva's disappointment, the food, when it came, consisted of sandwiches: pale pink slices of pressed ham or tinned salmon, interred between thin slices of tasteless white bread. Reluctantly, he put one of the salmon ones on his plate and took a bite. The briny taste had a metallic edge to it.

Charlie Frobisher demolished four sandwiches before de Silva finished his first one. Prasanna and Nadar, obviously hungry enough to eat anything, were almost as fast. Comforting himself with the prospect that a good dinner would be waiting for him at Sunnybank that evening, de Silva tried one of the pressed ham sandwiches, then gave up. Frobisher and his two officers had fallen to discussing the recent cricket match between Nuala and Hatton. De Silva's eyelids drooped. A short nap would do no harm.

'Sir!'

His eyelids flew open, and he saw Prasanna's earnest face.

'Sorry to disturb you, Inspector,' said Frobisher smiling.

'I wasn't asleep. Just resting my eyes.' Hastily, he hauled himself to his feet. 'Well, shall we be off again?'

This time, they changed places, and de Silva took the area that Prasanna had searched in the morning. As far as he could tell, his sergeant had done a thorough job; nothing invited closer investigation. Leaning against a wild mango tree for a rest, he watched a striped squirrel nibbling at one of the fruits then cracking the kernel. It was surprising that an animal so dainty, with its delicate paws and almost-translucent pink ears had such powerful teeth, but he knew from the damage the ones that came to the garden at Sunnybank inflicted that it was the case.

He shook himself. This was no time for ruminating. He'd better get back to the halfway hut.

Walking back, he blinked at the slanting rays of the sun. The party gathered at the hut was a gloomy one. 'I'm afraid I've not been much help to you,' said Frobisher as de Silva reached them.

'At least we will have eliminated one place.'

'Shall I report to the boss?'

'That would be most kind.'

'What will you do now?'

De Silva pondered the question. If the caddy was in the jungle, whether dead or alive, surely, they would have found him by now? There was no shame giving up. The thought of a good dinner too was suddenly making him feel lighter in heart than he had all day. Also, Jane might have some fresh ideas.

'Go home,' he said. 'I think we may as well all do the same.' He turned to Prasanna and Nadar. 'But I'm afraid this means your Sunday leave is cancelled. Tomorrow, you'd better start making enquiries around town.'

The young men looked rather downcast.

'I'll find out if there are any photographs of the caddy,' said Frobisher. 'Sometimes the club organises group ones.'

'That would be a great help. If he wants to disappear, he may use a different name, but his real one would be useful too.'

Frobisher nodded. 'Before we go, shall we take a last look inside the halfway hut? Just in case we missed a clue.'

De Silva didn't hold out much hope, but he agreed.

'There's no need for all of us to go in though,' he said. 'You and Nadar stay out here, Prasanna.'

The heat inside the halfway hut was even more oppressive than it had been out in the jungle. While he waited for Frobisher to check the small kitchen and scullery area, de Silva used his handkerchief to wipe a clean circle in the dust coating the window. It let in more light and he looked around the room; no clues jumped out at him. It surprised him that the building was still standing. Some of the cracks in the wall were deep enough to fit a man's hand. He was just thinking that they reminded him of a cave painting in one of Jane's books that showed a group of spindly-legged men hunting a deer, when Frobisher called out.

'Come and look at this!'

In the scullery area, through the window behind the sink, de Silva saw something. At first, it appeared to be a dark blanket draped over a metal tank. No, it was moving; it was a thick layer of flies.

'That must be where water was stored,' said Frobisher. 'But I suspect the flies are interested in more than stagnant water. I think we may have found what we're looking for after all.'

CHAPTER 9

'How horrible.'

Jane shuddered when de Silva told her how they found the caddy.

'What did you do?' she asked.

'Hauled his body out of the water tank – not a pleasant task. I was glad I had young Frobisher and Prasanna with me. They're both strong, and luckily, they have the stomach for that kind of thing. I'm afraid poor Nadar went quite green and had to disappear into the bushes.' He smiled ruefully. 'I think a desk job suits him better than the gritty nitty of policing.'

'Nitty-gritty, dear.'

'Hmm.' He took a sip of his mango juice. 'In any case, Frobisher and Prasanna collected branches and managed to construct a makeshift stretcher out of those and a piece of old tarpaulin they found in the halfway hut. Between them, they moved the caddy's body onto it, then Frobisher drove to the clubhouse and telephoned the undertakers. We waited until they came.'

'What will happen to it?'

'We managed to talk to Archie. It's unusual, but in the circumstances, he confirmed that the Residence will pay for a suitable funeral.'

'Who else have you told?'

'Mark Brodie. He was the only member of the committee up at the club.'

One of the servants appeared in the doorway to the verandah. 'Dinner is ready, memsahib.'

'Thank you, Logu. We'll come in.'

'We had another interesting find,' said de Silva, shaking out his napkin and putting it in his lap.

'What was that, dear?'

'Something like a glove, or rather a mitten.'

'For a man's hand or a woman's, would you say?'

'Neither. It was heavily padded and made of leather. Frobisher told me it would be used to protect the head of a wooden golf club.'

'Did you find it in the tank?'

'No, just off the path between where we found Harvey's body and the halfway hut. The killer wouldn't have had a cover on his club when he attacked Harvey, so if this one did belong to him, it might have fallen out of his pocket as he left the scene or was carrying the caddy's body to the hut. There were teeth marks in the leather and a lot of the stuffing had fallen out.' He raised an eyebrow. 'That's probably in the nest of some bird by now. I imagine an animal with sharp teeth like a civet or a mongoose got hold of it and chewed it for a while then lost interest.'

'So you think it would have belonged to the killer rather than Bernard Harvey?'

'Yes. Frobisher checked that all the covers he would expect to see were present and correct in Harvey's bag. Then again, another golfer entirely might have lost it on the course and an animal carried it off.'

He spooned a mound of fluffy rice onto his plate and added a generous helping of runner beans fragrant with curry leaves, turmeric, ginger and coconut. Next, he took some jackfruit curry and a spoonful of squash that had been simmered with lime juice and coconut milk. Adding some beetroot pickle, he began to eat.

'At least the find hasn't spoiled your appetite, dear.'

'Not much does,' he said cheerfully, but in truth, the discovery had been sobering. It didn't prove conclusively that the caddy was innocent – he might have had an accomplice who turned on him – but his death had been a brutal one. On the way home, he had decided to spare Jane all the grim details.

'If this cover has nothing to do with the crime, it would be useful to establish who it does belong to,' said Jane.

'With the state it's in, I doubt anyone will recognise it.'

'They might remember losing one though.'

'True, but if I get Mark Brodie or Charlie Frobisher to enquire, people may start asking questions.'

'Where is it now?'

De Silva forked up some of his rice and jackfruit curry and put it in his mouth. 'In the Morris,' he said when he had swallowed. 'I'll show it to you after we've eaten.'

* * *

After dinner, de Silva went out to the Morris. Standing on the drive, he looked up at the night sky: a dark, velvet canopy scattered with stars. The air was still warm; he wished he had nothing else to do that evening but sit and enjoy it with Jane.

Back on the verandah, he put the bag with the club cover inside on the table, fished the cover out and held it up. It was a sorry remnant of its former self: the leather ripped and pitted with teeth marks. Picking it up, Jane peered into what was left of the lining. 'If the owner's name was on it, it's likely that's where it would be.' She looked more closely. 'It's hard to make out, but there is something here.'

'It's probably just the maker's name,' de Silva said pessimistically. He didn't have high hopes that the search party had found a vital piece of evidence.

'Perhaps you're right.'

She put the cover down. 'What Mark Brodie had to say about the perimeter fence doesn't narrow the field very much.'

'Unfortunately, it doesn't. I suppose I might ask Brodie to let me see the club's membership records. Prasanna or Nadar could go through them to see who's still a member from the days when the halfway hut was in use. It may not help, but it's something to keep in mind.'

'You say it was obvious that the treasurer, Llewellyn, didn't like Bernard Harvey.'

'Yes, but it's hard to imagine him having the stomach for murder, let alone such a violent one. He seemed a glum, ineffectual character.'

'Some people said the same of Dr Crippen.'

De Silva smiled.

'Very true. Well, tomorrow I'll find out what Mr Duncan has to say for himself. From what I hear, he's a tougher character altogether.'

CHAPTER 10

Jane had arranged for a friend to give her a lift home from church the following morning, and she hadn't returned by the time de Silva set off for the Duncans' bungalow.

The road mounted higher into the hills; a cool breeze freshened the air. Momentarily, the magnificent views over slopes clad with green vistas of tea bushes distracted him. After a while, he wondered if he had missed the turning to the bungalow. Just as he was debating whether to turn around, he saw the sign. Drawing up at the gates, he waited for the guard to emerge from his hut and let the Morris through.

The drive sloped upwards, with an overgrown rockery on the right-hand side that was divided from it by a wide gully. Flights of winding steps were visible amongst the vegetation. The feature might have had charm once. What a pity it was so obviously neglected.

The bungalow that eventually came into view was extensive – Tom Duncan's legal practice must be a successful one. It was painted white with green shutters and, like the Harvey place, had a loggia running along its frontage, but it wasn't embellished with plants.

A servant answered the door and showed de Silva into the large drawing room that led off the hall. Invited to take a seat, he sat gingerly on one of the green-plush sofas. Oil paintings hung on the walls, that were, de Silva guessed from their similarity to those at the Residence, of the Scottish Highlands. An uncomfortable feeling settled over him. The room was neither cosy nor elegant; it gave off an aura of oppressive gloom.

Five minutes passed before he heard footsteps in the hall and the door opened. He jumped to his feet.

The woman who walked in was attractive but also had an air of sadness about her. De Silva estimated that she was in her early forties. Her hair was blonde, and her cream linen skirt and silk blouse revealed a slim figure.

She gave him a nervous smile. 'Good afternoon, Inspector. I'm Ella Duncan. I'm afraid my husband's still suffering with a bad back. We never went to church in the end. He got up later than he originally intended this morning, and he's just finishing dressing. Can I offer you some tea while you wait?'

'Thank you, but no.'

After Ella Duncan had left him, he wondered how much she knew. Presumably, her husband had told her something, for she seemed unsurprised by his arrival. She was no Jane though. In Ella Duncan's place, Jane would have been full of questions.

He started to look around the room. The furnishings were heavy and masculine; the only note of warmth came from a fine Indian rug that glowed against the dark wood of the teak floor. Two framed photographs on a side table attracted his attention. In one of them, a stunningly attractive young woman stood beside an open-topped automobile. De Silva wasn't sure, but he suspected the car was an early model of a Hispano-Suiza from before the Great War.

The other photograph showed a well-dressed, attractive couple standing with a young boy and two little girls. One was very pretty and looked to be a younger version of the stunning young woman beside the car. The other squinted into the sun, her plain features unimproved by a fierce scowl. They stood in front of a whitewashed, palm-frond roofed bungalow. In the background, he saw tea terraces. It might have been somewhere in Ceylon, but he doubted it. There was something about the scene that looked wrong for his country. Also there was a faint line of mountains in the blue distance that he didn't recognise. Maybe the photograph had been taken up in the tea country in the north of India. He'd heard it was more mountainous there.

The door opened and he turned, expecting to see Duncan, but it was his wife once again.

'I'm sorry, Inspector. My husband won't keep you much longer.'

'That's quite alright, ma'am. I have been admiring your beautiful rug. Was it bought in India?'

For the first time, Ella Duncan looked a little more animated. 'Yes, and I take great pleasure in it. The rest of the furnishings in the house belonged to my husband before we married. But I'm sure you haven't come to discuss our decorations, Inspector. I suppose you want to talk to my husband about Bernard Harvey.'

'Yes, ma'am. Did you know him well?'

'I—'

The door opened and a tall man, walking with the aid of a stick, came in. A slight stoop, perhaps due to his back problem, detracted from his height. With his prominent nose, deep-set eyes and thin lips, he had a disconcerting air. If he was the boy in the photograph, the years had robbed his face of its look of lively enthusiasm. It was hard to tell his age. It was possible he was younger than he looked.

'Good afternoon, Inspector de Silva. I'm Tom Duncan. Forgive me for keeping you waiting.' Duncan turned to his wife. 'I expect you have matters to attend to, my dear. You'll excuse my wife, Inspector, won't you?'

It was more a statement than a question.

Ella Duncan looked abashed. 'If you're sure, Inspector. I am rather busy.'

'Certainly, ma'am, but I may have a few questions for you later.'

'Very well.'

The door closed behind her.

'Thank you, Inspector,' said Duncan. 'My wife suffers with her nerves, and I prefer to shield her from unpleasantness. Once again, my apologies for delaying you. I hope you aren't in a hurry to be off anywhere else.'

Only back to town for my lunch, thought de Silva. Out loud, he said, 'No need for an apology, sir. I'm sorry to disturb you when you're indisposed.'

'No matter. Won't you sit down?'

Duncan moved stiffly to a capacious leather armchair on one side of the fireplace and indicated that de Silva should take the one opposite. Jane, he reflected, would have brightened the empty grate with an arrangement of flowers.

'It probably does me good to walk a little,' Duncan remarked as he sat down. He covered his mouth with his hand to suppress a dry cough. 'My wife tends to make a greater fuss than is necessary about my infirmities. Are you married, Inspector?'

'I am, sir.'

'Then perhaps you know what I mean.'

He rested his stick against the arm of his chair. 'Well, Brodie's told me something about this unfortunate affair, but I understand you're here to fill me in. Shall we get on with it?'

He listened carefully while de Silva explained the circumstances of Bernard Harvey's death. It was hard to read his expression. There was certainly no flicker of sorrow or distress in the lawyer's eyes.

'A bad business,' he remarked when de Silva came to the end of his story. 'I won't say Bernard Harvey and I were close friends, but I acted for him for many years. I presume you already know that I was his solicitor.'

De Silva nodded. 'When did you last see Mr Harvey, sir?'

Duncan pondered for a few moments. 'If you need a precise answer to that question, I'll have to ask my secretary to check my office diary. Offhand, I'd say it was Monday or Tuesday of last week. He wanted some advice on a project in which he was considering investing.'

'Did he seem worried about anything? Different from his usual self in any way?'

'Not that I noticed. What are you getting at, Inspector?'

'Some men make enemies in business. If that was the case, as you're his solicitor, he might have confided in you.'

Shifting slightly in his seat, Duncan shook his head. 'Bernard Harvey drove a hard bargain and didn't like being bested by the people he had dealings with, but I doubt he aroused murderous feelings in any of his business associates. Are you certain that the motive isn't more obvious, Inspector? Could it be a case of a theft that went wrong? I believe his caddy is missing.'

'Not any longer, sir. We found his body yesterday. He had also been murdered. But theft seems unlikely in any case. Mr Harvey's gold watch and wallet were still there.'

'Hmm, I take your point. Regrettable news about the caddy.'

'I understand you didn't take part in the lunch for the American ambassador.'

'I had a prior engagement in Hatton.' Duncan grimaced. 'Probably the drive on these wretched roads didn't help my back.'

'May I ask what it was?'

'A lunchtime meeting with a major client of mine at my office. You're welcome to verify that. I worked at home in the morning until about midday, then left to drive there.' If this proved to be true, it put Duncan beyond suspicion.

'You look perturbed, Inspector. I assure you, the last

thing I want is to lose an important client. Harvey's grandson, Jack, stands to inherit, but I've no idea whether he'll decide to remain a client of my firm. Unfortunately, we have our competitors.'

'Is there anyone who can confirm the time you left home, sir?'

'My wife. I expect you'd like to speak to her before you go.'

'Thank you.'

A wife wasn't the most reliable of witnesses, but then Duncan didn't look to be in any state to attack and kill a man.

'Are Elizabeth and Jack still at the house?' asked Duncan.

'As far as I know, they are, sir.'

'I delayed sending our condolences; one doesn't want to intrude at such a time, but I ought not to leave it too much longer before speaking with them. Of course, when the initial shock is over, there'll be decisions to make and a great deal to do.'

He frowned. 'I'm glad to say, that to the best of my knowledge, nothing like this has occurred before in the annals of the golf club. I'm sure I speak for the committee when I say I hope it stays under wraps. One doesn't want to spread alarm, does one? Fear of a killer who strikes at random and so forth.'

'Do you have reason to think the attack was a random one, sir?'

'I didn't say that, Inspector. To be frank, I have absolutely no idea. Equally, I have no idea who would want Bernard Harvey dead.'

'Would you say that Jack Harvey and his grandfather got on?'

'I don't deal in conjecture. All I can tell you is that I never saw them argue.'

'Did he ever tell you that he intended to cut Jack out of his will?'

'Has someone suggested he threatened to do so?'

'I'd rather not divulge that at this stage, sir.'

'No, I don't expect you would,' said Duncan dryly.

De Silva was reminded that Duncan was still the family's solicitor. For as long as that was the case, he was bound to be careful what he said.

'In the heat of the moment, many men say things they don't mean,' Duncan went on. 'I don't recall Bernard Harvey speaking in those terms, but he may have voiced his frustrations with his grandson to others. I imagine it's not news to you that Jack Harvey isn't what one would describe as a chip off the old block.'

'No, sir. Several people have intimated that his dedication to business is somewhat lacking.'

A bark of laughter escaped Duncan's throat. 'Nicely put, Inspector. But Jack wouldn't be the first young man to take time to settle down.'

'Indeed.'

Duncan reached for his stick and stood up, then poked at the bell on the wall near his chair. 'You wanted to speak to my wife. I'll tell one of the servants to fetch her.'

A few moments elapsed before the door opened and Ella Duncan herself walked in.

'Ah, my dear. The inspector would like to hear from you what time I left home on Friday for Hatton.'

'Of course. My husband left at midday, Inspector. He had a lunchtime meeting there.'

'There we are,' said Duncan. He went over to his wife and put an arm around her shoulders. 'I'm afraid I haven't been of much assistance to you, Inspector. But feel free to contact me if I can do anything else.'

'I will, sir.'

* * *

He could have driven to the Crown Hotel to find out if they would confirm that Elizabeth Harvey had lunched there on Friday as she claimed, but he decided to wait until the morning. Arriving on a sleepy Sunday afternoon would draw attention to his presence and he'd prefer not to do that. He would also keep the call to the Kandy police station for the morning. There would only be an emergency team on duty on a Sunday.

'Why don't you try to relax, dear?' asked Jane. 'You've made good progress already.'

'A long way to go still. But I expect you're right. It will do no harm to allow what we've found out so far time to settle in my mind.'

Out on the verandah, he settled down with the Saturday evening edition of the local newspaper which he'd not yet had a chance to read. News in Nuala was usually confined to topics that concerned the British community and was rarely of a dramatic nature, but this time, an article on the front page was headlined: *Sudden Death of Top Nuala Businessman.*

He sighed: there was no escape. The news had got out quickly. The editor of the *Nuala Evening News* must be a member of the golf club. De Silva scanned the article; fortunately there was no mention of murder. In a few days' time, the Kandy and, in view of Harvey's status in the business community, no doubt the Colombo newspapers would probably just reprint the story. If there was any fear that they would delve further, doubtless William Petrie would make it clear to their editors that he expected discretion.

De Silva yawned, there was something about Sunday afternoons that made one sleepy. Odd though, when he was faced with a murder case. But, unusually, he had the feeling of being disengaged from it. Was it because Archie Clutterbuck was too busy with the American visitors to be constantly wanting to be kept up to date? No, it wasn't that.

Far more likely that he was affected by the attitude of the Royal Nuala Golf Club. The club was so keen to stress its apartness that the murder seemed to have happened in a different world.

He shook himself. It was still his duty to investigate the crime. Looking up, he saw Jane standing in the doorway. 'Were you having a little doze, dear?' she asked with a smile.

He grinned. 'Thinking. I do it best with my eyes shut.'

CHAPTER 11

On Monday morning, Prasanna and Nadar were already at their desks when he arrived at the station. It was amazing the effect that being family men had on them. Gone were the days when they might have been found hiding away in the back yard, sneaking in some cricket practice. He no longer surprised Nadar quickly hiding some toy elephant or tiger he was whittling for his eldest son under his desk. With another boy to provide for now and Prasanna and his wife, Kuveni, with a daughter, promotion was probably much further forward in their minds than it used to be. Soon, he would have to look out for his own job.

Still, they deserved praise for their efforts on Saturday. In future, he would have to try and find them some more interesting duties, although nothing came to mind on the Harvey case that he wanted to delegate.

'You both did a good job on Saturday.'

'Thank you, sir,' said Prasanna. 'What would you like us to do now?'

'Hold the fort here for a while. I have to go up to the Crown Hotel. I need to check that Mrs Harvey had lunch there on Friday.' He paused. Since he didn't want an enquiry to cause comment, he hadn't given much thought to how he would approach the task.

Nadar brightened. 'One of my neighbours is a doorman at the Crown, sir. He and his wife are good friends of ours. If you want to ask discreetly, perhaps he can help.'

It wasn't such a bad idea. 'Are you sure he won't blab?'

'Absolutely, sir.'

'Well, in that case, I think it's in order for you and Prasanna to go.' He described Elizabeth Harvey and her car.

'Is there anything else, sir?' asked Prasanna.

De Silva thought of the Victoria Clinic. If it was so exclusive, it might be better to visit or telephone them himself at some point. The British had a way of being very off-putting with junior officers when they wanted to be. Goodness knows, they might give him the same treatment, but he was likely to have better luck than Prasanna and Nadar.

'No, that will do for now.'

Once they left on their errand, he went into his office and picked up the telephone to put in a call to Kandy. He waited a few moments before the operator's voice came back on the line. 'Connecting you, sir.'

The desk sergeant remembered him, and they exchanged a few pleasantries.

'I'm sorry, sir,' the sergeant said when de Silva asked to speak to the first of his old colleagues he had in mind for the favour. 'He's not on duty today.'

'What about Inspector Weerasinghe?'

'He's out on an investigation all day. Inspector Jayaratne is available. Perhaps he can help you. Shall I put you through?'

De Silva frowned as the image of Jayaratne rose in his mind: a short, skinny fellow with a pinched face, round spectacles, thinning hair and a toothbrush moustache. They had been at the Police Training College in Colombo together, and de Silva hadn't been keen on him then. Since those far-off days, he had come across him from time to time and had never been glad to see him. Jayaratne was pompous and fond of putting other people down. Anyway, de Silva would never entirely trust a man who looked as if he didn't enjoy his food. It was a pity there was no one better he could ask for help, but he wanted an answer today. There was nothing else for it.

'Please do that.'

'Ah, Inspector Jayaratne,' he said, adopting a jocular tone when Jayaratne's oleaginous voice came down the line. 'It's very good of you to take my call.'

'De Silva, my old friend! It's a pleasure. It must be — let me see — ten years since we met. How is life in that backwater of yours? It must be pleasant to idle away one's days in the Hill Country.' He laughed mirthlessly.

'And how is life in Kandy?' asked de Silva, ignoring the jibe.

'Busy; very busy. The big city, you know. There are so many very important cases to solve.'

De Silva refrained from remarking that the size of a place didn't necessarily dictate the nature of the crimes committed there. In any case, being proud of having many cases to solve was an odd attitude. Wasn't it an important aspect of police work that you deterred crime on your patch? Clearly, the years hadn't made Jayaratne any less of an ass. Nevertheless, he must be pleasant: he wanted the man's help.

'So,' Jayaratne went on, 'what can I do for you?' A hint of boredom drawled in his voice. De Silva pulled a pen and a pad of paper towards him and started to doodle a picture of a donkey with a human face that resembled Jayaratne's. As he explained the favour he wanted, he gave it a toothy grin, then added a sombrero and an enormous pair of spectacles.

'I'd be most grateful for your help,' he concluded. 'The drive from Nuala to Kandy is a long one, and even in my sleepy hill town, we have urgent matters to deal with on occasion.'

'Glad to help,' said Jayaratne breezily. 'There should

be a formal request, of course—' He paused, and de Silva groaned inwardly. 'But for an old friend, I'll send one of my men round there without one and tell him to report back to you. We in the big city are always happy to support our provincial colleagues.'

Gritting his teeth, de Silva thanked him profusely and put down the telephone receiver. He scrawled a flourish under his drawing, screwed it into a ball and tossed it into the wastepaper basket.

CHAPTER 12

Deciding to wait for Prasanna and Nadar to get back, he put in a call to verify Tom Duncan's alibi. After being passed to various people, he found out that Duncan had indeed had a meeting in Hatton at the time he said. If Duncan's wife had told the truth, that put her husband out of the picture.

The sound of voices and footsteps told him Prasanna and Nadar had returned. He went out to the public room to meet them. 'Good, you're back. What news do you have for me?'

'Constable Nadar's neighbour was on duty as we hoped, sir. He confirmed that the lady arrived at the hotel for lunch at half past twelve and didn't leave until half past two.'

'Did she have a driver?'

'No, sir, she drove herself. Constable Nadar's neighbour told us that she does so quite frequently when she comes to the hotel.'

'Did he notice anything out of the ordinary?'

Prasanna shook his head. 'The lady was very gracious as always.'

'Good work. Well, as you had to give up your Saturday afternoon, I think you may take a few hours off.'

A beaming smile came over Nadar's face. 'Thank you, sir. It is my little boy's fourth birthday today. He will be very happy I can be at home with him.'

'My goodness, it seems only yesterday that he was a

baby. Fourth birthday, eh? Then go and enjoy it and wish him a happy birthday from me.'

'Thank you, sir.'

When the young men had left, de Silva looked at the clock. The police station at Kandy was much busier than Nuala's but with luck they would send someone this morning. Rather than go out on any other business, he would wait for their call. He went back into his office to write up his notes on the case. It was good to have a few quiet moments to think through his impressions so far.

First, Harvey's widow, Elizabeth, and the grandson, Jack. So far, her alibi was sound, although he still needed to make enquiries at the Victoria Clinic. However, he doubted even more now that he would find anything amiss. It was not only hard to credit that such an elegant, fastidious lady had committed such a brutal double murder, it was also hard to believe that she would, within the space of a few hours, arrive at the Crown Hotel looking as if nothing had happened.

De Silva found Jack harder to read: a privileged young man who, by several accounts, lacked drive and ambition, he also seemed to lack rivals. There was his grandfather's threat to disinherit him, but Mark Brodie had dismissed it as nothing more than an outburst of irritation on Bernard Harvey's part, nothing to be taken seriously. While not admitting to seeing anything specific, Tom Duncan had indicated much the same thing.

He considered the committee members who had known that Harvey was up at the course that morning: Mark Brodie, David Llewellyn, Tom Duncan, and Archie. At least Archie could be discounted. He'd been occupied with entertaining the American ambassador.

What about the other three? It would be helpful to have someone independent to corroborate the alibi that Brodie and Llewellyn had given. As they claimed they had been at Llewellyn's house, his servants immediately sprang to mind, but de Silva had been caught out before by employers who forced their servants to lie for them.

It would be useful to see where Llewellyn's house was. De Silva recalled a photograph of a black Jaguar in Brodie's office. It was a car that people would notice. If he was right, did Llewellyn have neighbours who might have seen it that morning? Rolling his shoulders to ease the stiffness in them, he considered the three men.

Brodie presented a challenge. If he knew something, he was going to be a hard nut to crack. On the other hand, Llewellyn seemed so meek that a little pressure might be enough to make him talk.

Tom Duncan was more like Brodie. It was easy to see that his professional life had accustomed him to fending off questions and giving nothing away. He'd been pleasant enough at their encounter, but that might easily change if he was asked questions he didn't want to answer.

He was jotting down a few more notes when the telephone interrupted him. He picked it up. 'Inspector de Silva speaking.'

The voice at the end of the line didn't have Jayaratne's pompous tone. The caller was a young man, and he sounded nervous. 'Good afternoon, sir, I have a message for you from Inspector Jayaratne.'

'Yes?'

'He was sorry not to telephone you himself, sir, but he has been called to an important meeting.'

More likely he'd decided to go home for a long lunch.

'He told me to advise you that he sent someone to make inquiries at the Blue Cat club concerning the party you are interested in.'

There was a long pause, and de Silva drummed his fingers on his desk. 'Get to the point,' he said, somewhat testily. He was beginning to feel extremely hungry, and envious of Jayaratne who was probably sitting down to a feast of delicious dishes.

'What did the manager at the Blue Cat club have to say?'

'The party in question left at eleven o'clock on Thursday night, sir.'

Ears suddenly pricking up, de Silva let out a low whistle. 'Was he sure about that?'

'I… er… I think so, sir.'

'You *think* so? The answer is yes or no.'

'Sorry, sir. Yes, he was sure.' The young man's voice was abject, and a twinge of guilt went through de Silva. He had been a rookie policeman once. He mustn't take his hunger pangs out on this unfortunate young man.

'Never mind,' he went on in a kindlier tone. 'Please thank Inspector Jayaratne for me.'

'Will there be anything else, sir?'

'Not for the moment. I'll call if there is.'

He put down the receiver and finished writing his notes then lacing his fingers behind his head, contemplated this news with a frown. Jack Harvey had lied. It was potent evidence against him. What was he hiding? Was it that he had murdered his grandfather and the caddy? And was his stepmother in on it after all? He'd have to tread carefully. If Jack was guilty, and perhaps his stepmother too, the last thing he wanted to do at this stage was alarm them.

The telephone rang again. This time, the voice that came down the line was the familiar one of his boss, Archie Clutterbuck, the assistant government agent.

'De Silva?'

'Mr Clutterbuck. I wasn't expecting to hear from you today.'

'Managed to get away from the Americans for a few minutes, but I mustn't be long. You'd better tell me quickly what's been going on. Any progress?'

Briefly, de Silva explained about the news from the Blue Cat club.

'Hmm,' rumbled Archie when he had finished. 'I expect you'll be checking the information out yourself, but it doesn't sound good for the young fellow, even though we can't discount the possibility that there's an innocent explanation. You'd better get back to the Harveys' place, de Silva. See if you can find out where he is. Tread carefully.'

'I'll do my best, sir.'

'And call me when you get back. If I'm not available, ask for Frobisher.'

'I will, sir.'

De Silva replaced the receiver. He was hungry, and he hadn't eaten lunch. That was something he'd attend to before he went.

In the bazaar, he headed for his favourite vendor's usual pitch. The walk took him past stalls piled with sweet-scented mangoes, pineapples and bunches of green bananas. There were mounds of spiky rambutans, custard apples that looked like small grenades, and many more kinds of fruit. Other stalls displayed hairy mounds of coconuts, sacks of lentils and rice, baskets of vegetables, and great bunches of coriander and other herbs, already wilting in the early afternoon heat.

He had loved the bazaar ever since he was a little boy and been allowed to go with his mother to shop there. The colours and smells, the vibrant, teeming life always raised his spirits: women browsing the stalls or carrying their shopping in straw baskets; men with bundles and baskets balanced on their heads; half-naked children running about among the crowds, and dogs and cats scavenging for discarded produce.

In the shade of a loggia that ran along the side of one of the Dutch-style buildings that were a feature of Nuala, groups of old men lounged in the shade, chewing paan and cackling with laughter. At the next junction of lanes, a gaudily painted statue of the Virgin Mary gazed down in silent adoration at the chubby baby lying on a bed of straw. Incongruously, a statue of the Buddha sat serenely nearby. This was a different world to the restrained, sober one of the Royal Nuala Golf Club – even if, de Silva thought wryly, the impression of orderly respectability that the club liked to project was currently proving to be a thin veneer.

He found the stall and, fortified by some kottu roti, the popular mixture of chopped flatbread mashed with eggs and vegetables, returned to the police station. In the small washroom at the back of the building, he combed his hair and straightened his tie. Right: he was ready. Quashing a slight feeling of apprehension at what awaited him, he went out to the Morris.

* * *

At the Harveys' bungalow, the Rolls Royce Phantom was again parked on the drive, but there was no sign of the SSI Tourer. As he passed the Rolls, he thought once more how much he would love to have the time to admire the splendid car in greater detail, but duty called.

He rang the doorbell and waited for the sound of footsteps. Soon, a servant arrived.

'Are the memsahib and Mr Harvey in?'

'Only the memsahib is at home, sahib, but—'

De Silva interrupted him. 'Please tell her I would like to speak with her.'

The servant nodded and backed into the shadows of the hall to let him in.

There was no one in the elegant drawing room he and Frobisher had walked through to meet Elizabeth Harvey on the evening of her husband's death. The servant went to the verandah doors and indicated that de Silva should follow him into the garden.

Once again, now was not the time, but as he emerged into the sunshine, de Silva thought how much he would enjoy exploring it. There were too many pleasures to take in quickly. Beyond a stone-paved terrace, an immaculately mown lawn made a splash of green, contrasting with flowerbeds crammed with bright flowers. The glitter of blue water caught his eye. So, as well as all these delights, the Harveys owned a swimming pool. The servant led him over to it.

Shaded by a large parasol, Elizabeth Harvey sat by the water. A navy swimsuit trimmed with white hugged her slim, tanned figure. The fashion magazine that lay open in her lap and the cool drink on the small table at her elbow added to a picture of relaxation that jarred with her recently bereaved state. She looked up from her magazine as de Silva and the servant approached. Her dark glasses prevented him from reading the expression in her eyes.

'Why, Inspector, good afternoon. I didn't expect to see you back so quickly. It's so hot, I decided to spend the afternoon down here. May I offer you something cool to drink?' She reached for her glass, and ice clinked.

For a moment, her calmness disconcerted de Silva. Then he reflected that it might be an act to protect her from the unwelcome curiosity or sympathy of others, rather than evidence of indifference to her husband's death.

'Thank you, ma'am, that's most kind of you, but I won't stay long. I'm sorry to disturb you again at such a time.'

She lowered her dark glasses and looked at him over the top of the frames. 'I suppose it's too much to hope for that you've come to tell me my husband's body may be released to us. Jack and I would like to arrange his funeral. It will be hard to move on until that's done,' she added with a sigh.

Guilt that he hadn't considered the family's need to

give Harvey a fitting send-off came over de Silva. There was really no reason to delay that. 'I must apologise again, ma'am. I'll see to it that the necessary instructions are given.'

'Thank you. Now, I'm sure you had another purpose in coming. I'm afraid I doubt that I'll be able to illuminate the situation for you any more clearly than at our last meeting. Try as I might, I've been unable to think of anyone my husband had dealings with who disliked him enough to commit murder.'

'Actually, ma'am, it was your stepson I hoped to speak with.'

'Jack? I'm afraid you've missed him. He was here at lunchtime. You might find him at the factory. He mentioned something about going down to have a word with our manager, Peter Hancock. If you wish to go there, one of the servants can take you. But I doubt Jack has anything to add either. We're both convinced that my husband was the victim of a robbery. Either at the hands of his caddy, or with the wretched man's connivance. I hope it won't be long before he's found and confesses to his crime.'

'The caddy has been found, ma'am.'

'Has he confessed?'

'I'm afraid there's no question of that, ma'am. The man was dead when we found him. Murdered.'

Elizabeth Harvey took a sharp breath. 'But how can you be sure there was no attempt at robbery? What if he had an accomplice? The caddy might have lost his nerve and the accomplice killed him then ran away.'

'Robbery seems unlikely considering the valuable items we found on your late husband's body, ma'am. They will be returned to you, of course,' he added quickly. 'In the meantime, I just need a little more information about your stepson's visit to Kandy on Thursday. Merely to complete the record, you understand.'

If Elizabeth Harvey found his explanation suspicious, she didn't betray her doubts.

'Very well, Inspector.' She picked up the small bell on the table at her side and rang it. To de Silva's relief, they didn't have long to wait before the same servant who had shown him in returned.

'Inspector de Silva wishes to go to the factory. Find someone to show him the way.'

'Yes, memsahib.'

She turned back to de Silva. 'Why don't you go out by the garden, Inspector? It will be quicker. And thank you for your understanding about poor Bernard's body. Waiting is very hard.'

Did he imagine it or was there a gleam of moisture in her dark eyes? He felt a twinge of pity for her. Surely, she was innocent? Why would she want to lose an adoring husband and an enviable life?

'Please rest assured, ma'am, you won't have to wait much longer.'

He followed the servant across the lawn and around the side of the house. Drawing level with a break in the trees, he noticed the splendid view over plantation terraces that stretched into the distance until emerald green faded to dusky blue. That must be where he was being taken to.

A low cough reminded him that the servant was waiting. He mustn't dawdle. It didn't project a professional air. Yet he couldn't resist a last glance at the garden he had just left. Elizabeth Harvey was still by the pool, but she had not gone back to reading her magazine. Instead, she sat on her sun lounger, staring out across the garden, apparently lost in thought.

CHAPTER 13

Down at the factory, a tall man with a deeply tanned, leathery face was shouting orders to the gang of workers unloading straw panniers filled with fresh tea leaves from the backs of donkeys. In the shade of a long tin shed, women in faded saris were already busy sorting the first loads. Dust hung in the hot air, making de Silva's throat itch and his eyes smart. He feared these factories were not pleasant places to work, although this one looked a little better than some he had seen. He noticed a water trough where some of the male workers were sluicing dust from their faces and bodies, presumably having finished their tasks. The women chattered like a flock of starlings as their fingers flashed through the leaves.

The tall man broke off from what he was doing and walked over to de Silva, his blue eyes squinting ferociously against the sun. He looked to be in his late forties, not handsome like Mark Brodie, but with a certain rugged attraction. De Silva imagined that it might appeal to some women. His dun-coloured shirt showed dark patches of sweat and he wore a faded canvas hat, stained by years of exposure to the dirt and dust of a tea factory.

'What can I do for you, Inspector?' he asked gruffly.

'I'd like to speak to Mr Hancock.'

'You're talking to him. I assume this is about Bernard Harvey.'

'Is there somewhere we can be private?'

Hancock glanced at his workers. 'Carry on with your tasks. And no slacking.' He turned back to de Silva. 'We'll go to my office. It's this way.'

Glad of a respite from the dust of the sorting yard, de Silva followed Hancock into the building and up several flights of wooden stairs. On the first floor, there was a long, shadowy room fitted out with tanks. He presumed that was where the leaves were dried. Higher up, they passed numerous storerooms before Hancock stopped at a door. In script faded with age, the glass panel that filled the top half displayed the word "Manager".

'Come in and take a seat.' Hancock gestured to a chair on one side of a large wooden desk. Sitting down opposite de Silva, he didn't remove his hat. 'Under the circumstances, I imagine you may be surprised to find everything proceeding in the normal way down here, but the business has to go on. We have our regular shipments to send out. In particular, a large one in a couple of days.'

There was no hint of defensiveness in Hancock's voice. De Silva suspected that life would have gone on as usual for him even if there hadn't been shipments to prepare for. Whether that was because of his nature, or because he disliked his late boss, it was hard to say without knowing the man better. The information he had so far indicated that although Harvey was a difficult man to work for, Hancock was of a phlegmatic temperament that could handle an abrasive superior. 'I understand, sir. Just for the record, were you at work here on Friday?'

'I was. I had a meeting with an agent up from Colombo in the morning and a shipment being sent off in the afternoon to a Colombo exporter. You're welcome to look at the books and my appointment diary if you wish. You'll find the relevant telephone numbers and the names of the men I dealt with written down there.'

'Thank you, I'll do that before I go.'

'Have you been up to see Elizabeth?'

'I've just come from her.'

'I've done my best to reassure her that I'll keep everything on track for the moment. Do you have any idea when the body will be released? I know she and Jack are anxious to arrange Harvey's funeral.'

'We spoke about that. I'll see it's done as soon as possible.'

'Good. At least that'll be one thing off their minds, but there'll be a lot of decisions to be made once the dust has settled.'

De Silva frowned. 'It was my understanding that Mr Jack Harvey would take over his grandfather's business.'

Hancock raised an eyebrow. 'That's the theory, but in practice, Jack will listen to Elizabeth. Don't let the glamour fool you, Inspector. Elizabeth Harvey has a sharp brain.'

This wasn't the impression that Mark Brodie had given him. Brodie had been dismissive of Elizabeth's abilities and her interest in the business, save for the fact that it provided her with the luxuries she liked. Which portrayal of her character was the true one?

'Do you intend to stay on?'

For the first time, Hancock smiled, revealing surprisingly white teeth. 'If I'm asked to.'

'Have you worked at the plantation for many years?'

'Coming up for ten.'

'Then you knew Mr Harvey pretty well.'

Hancock shrugged. 'I wouldn't say that necessarily. I'm not part of the golf club or his social set, but we'd built up a good working relationship. Provided the profits kept rolling in, he let me get on with the work my way.'

'And did they?'

'This is one of the most successful plantations in the Hill Country.'

'As far as you're aware, did he make an enemy of anyone with whom he did business?'

'I'm afraid that if you're hoping I'll come up with a likely suspect, Inspector, you're going to be disappointed. Harvey was a tough operator, but he played with a straight bat. People may not have warmed to him, but they respected him.'

'You said you've worked at this plantation for nearly ten years. Before that, were you working elsewhere in this area?'

'No, I was in Malaysia, planting rubber. But after a few years, the climate got to me. I'd heard good things about Ceylon and decided to give it a try. I got a job at a plantation north of here, but there was little prospect of advancement. I came across Bernard Harvey at one of the tea auctions in Colombo. He'd recently married Elizabeth and wanted a manager to take over some of the day-to-day running of the business. We settled on a handshake that he'd give me a six months' trial.' He gestured to the office around him. 'As you see, I'm still here.'

'When did Jack Harvey join the business?'

'Let me see… it's nearly three years ago. Before that he was in England for a time. Harvey insisted on his being educated there. Eton College, naturally. Only the best would do. I'm afraid, however, that Jack was never going to be a scholar. Harvey pulled strings to get him a place at Oxford afterwards, but he was sent down before he graduated. There was "an incident" apparently, but I've never got to the bottom of what happened.'

'Despite that, would you say that Mr Harvey was fond of his grandson?'

'I would, even though he often found him exasperating. All the same, he confided in me once or twice that he believed Jack would turn the corner and make something of himself in the end.'

It was hard to imagine anyone confiding in Peter Hancock, especially if that man was Bernard Harvey, but perhaps he had recognised a rough integrity in his manager that engendered trust. After all, one day Hancock might well be the one to play an important role in steering Jack onto the straight and narrow.

'If he's here, I'd like a word with him.'

'I'm afraid he's not, and I haven't seen him all day.'

'Do you have any idea where I'll find him?'

Hancock shrugged. 'You must understand, his grandfather's death will have hit him hard. I suspect he wants to be alone.'

'Is there a particular place in Nuala that you think he would go to?'

'I doubt he'd go to the Crown or any of the other British haunts. You might try the Mackenzie Road area.'

De Silva knew the area. It was a part of town where there were numerous small bars favoured by the less desirable citizens of Nuala. Peter Hancock looked at him shrewdly. 'I can guess what you're thinking. Why does he want to go to such a rat hole? All I can assume is that it's something to do with the rebellious streak in him. Perhaps he'll get over it now he hasn't got his grandfather to rebel against. I sincerely hope so, or it won't make running the plantation any easier.'

De Silva stood up. 'Thank you for your time. I'll take those names and telephone numbers now if I may.'

Hancock produced the appointment diary and de Silva wrote them down.

He returned to the Morris and bumped his way along the plantation's dusty road until he reached the main one back into town. As he drove, Hancock faded from his mind, replaced by thoughts of what Jack Harvey would have to say for himself. It was a pity he had to venture into Mackenzie Road to look for him. Glancing at the sun, he wished there were more daylight left, but it couldn't be helped.

* * *

Back at the station, to de Silva's surprise, Sergeant Prasanna's bicycle was once more chained up outside. Inside, he found the young man with his head bent over some paperwork.

'I didn't expect to see you back today. What have you got there?'

'The traffic accidents for last month, sir. I am checking that all the fines have been paid.'

Traffic accidents, most of which involved collisions between rickshaws and the cows that wandered the town's roads, were frequent in Nuala. The fines levied on offenders were a lucrative source of revenue for the British authorities.

'Your enthusiasm is praiseworthy, but I'm surprised you prefer dealing with traffic violations to an afternoon at home.'

Prasanna pulled a face. 'My mother is visiting, sir. She and my wife, Kuveni, like to find jobs in the house that they say I am neglecting. If they knew I had the afternoon off, they would give me no peace.'

'Ah, I see. In any case, it's lucky for me you came back.' Swiftly, he explained about Jack. 'We'll go straight off,' he finished. 'I'd like to try and get there before dark. No point courting trouble.'

'Yes, sir,' said Prasanna, a touch nervously.

In his office, de Silva took his Webley from a drawer in his desk. If Jack was at Mackenzie Road and had friends who came to his aid, it might be advisable for him and Prasanna to have greater protection than their fists.

He decided to leave the Morris at the station. Out in the street, he hailed a rickshaw and told the driver to take them to Mackenzie Road. 'Double your usual fare,' de Silva said firmly when the man looked dubious.

'Are you sure Jack Harvey will be there, sir?' asked Prasanna warily. 'What will we do if we find him?'

'Invite him to come to the police station and explain himself.'

De Silva looked sideways and saw that his young sergeant sat right on the edge of his seat. He tapped his shoulder. 'Don't worry, I'm sure the two of us will be more than a match for him.'

'It's not that I'm worried about, sir. There are many bad types in Mackenzie Road.'

'Hmm.'

They fell silent as the rickshaw man drove them past the bazaar. Most of the stallholders had packed up for the day. The unsold produce they had left behind them was rapidly being demolished by the local monkeys and stray cats and dogs. De Silva smelt the pungent aroma of fruit and vegetables spoiled by the heat.

As they neared Mackenzie Road, the rickshaw driver grumbled at the large number of potholes he had to avoid. People by the roadside cast suspicious glances in their direction as they went by. De Silva began to have doubts. Would they really find Jack Harvey in this insalubrious place? For a wealthy young man, he must have some strange friends if he risked visiting it. Was it due to rebelliousness, or the attraction of a place where he would have almost no chance of encountering the respectable members of the British community? Or was there more to it than that? Over de Silva's years in Nuala, there had been a few violent crimes in the district. If one wanted to do away with an enemy, Mackenzie Road would be the place to find a willing accomplice.

Despite de Silva's hopes, it was nearly dark when they reached their destination. He paid off the rickshaw driver who barely paused to acknowledge the generous tip, pedalling away so fast that de Silva could have sworn he saw steam spurting from the man's grimy heels.

At this early hour of the evening, Mackenzie Road was

still reasonably quiet. The first bar they tried was almost deserted. In the next, a noisy group of men drinking beer were the only customers. They spoke in English and de Silva guessed from their clothes that they were workers from the construction site to the west of Nuala where a road washed away in last season's monsoon was being rebuilt. Satisfied that Jack Harvey wasn't there, they moved on to the next bar along the street. What was it that Jane always said? Third time lucky? But it didn't work on this occasion.

De Silva ran his tongue round his dry lips. He was beginning to think fondly of a cold drink, but he wasn't keen on beer. In any case, drinking on duty wouldn't set Prasanna a good example. Instead, he stopped by a stall that was selling coconut milk and paid a few annas for two bowls of the sweet, creamy liquid. Its fragrance and the fresh taste revived him.

'Drink up,' he said briskly.

'Yes, sir.' As he drained his bowl, Prasanna's chestnut eyes appeared above the rim, his gaze roving uneasily up and down the street.

They returned the wooden bowls to the curious stall-holder. He probably thinks there's going to be a bit of excitement this evening, thought de Silva. If they found Jack Harvey, he might be right, for the more de Silva considered it, the more he doubted that Harvey would come quietly.

Investigating a succession of bars, interspersed with cheap eating houses, massage parlours, and barber's shops, took up the next hour. The smell of hair oil, curry, and open drains assailed de Silva's sensitive nose.

At the entrance to the final bar they came to, a hulking man who looked to have started drinking early staggered out of the dark interior, cannoning into de Silva. The hulk swore and bunched his fists, then noticing their badges, thought better of starting a fight and slunk off into the darkness.

'My goodness, that was close, sir,' said Prasanna under his breath.

'Yes, we don't want to cause a commotion before we've even found Jack Harvey.' He peered around the room. It was hot and airless, inadequately lit by a few kerosene lamps that added their oily smell to the pungent odours of cheap tobacco and unwashed bodies. As his eyes became accustomed to the gloom, he saw a table not far from the door where four men were playing cards, watched by a gaggle of onlookers shouting advice. In a far corner, another group played darts. A long wooden bar, stained treacle-brown, took up the length of the room. On the wall behind it hung a mirror that had lost much of its silvering, leaving it peppered with black. Its lower half reflected shelves of bottles of all sizes. Surely a man like Jack Harvey who could afford the Crown Hotel wasn't going to be found here? But then Peter Hancock had said that the luxurious hotel favoured by the British was the last place Jack would go in the present situation.

A hush descended on the room; de Silva realised that he and Prasanna were being watched. If Jack was there, he had probably noticed them too, or if not, he soon would. What would his reaction be? If he was guilty, might he try to make a run for it? Or would he stay and brazen the encounter out?

A man sat on one of the stools pulled up to the bar. His back was turned to them, but his build and hair looked right for Jack Harvey. De Silva took a deep breath. 'I think that's him over there,' he muttered to Prasanna. 'The fellow on the fifth barstool from the left.'

'Are you going to arrest him straight away, sir?' Prasanna whispered back.

'Not yet. Wait until people get on with what they were doing. I want to attract as little attention as possible. With luck, we can persuade him to come with us without any fuss. I'll do the talking, but you must be ready to help me if he tries to run.'

His eyes roving around the room, de Silva saw a few men leave their tables and slip quietly away. It was their lucky night; he wasn't interested in them this time. The card players had already gone back to their game and darts were once more thudding into the board. The bar's clientele was already losing interest in their presence. He nudged Prasanna who seemed to have got over his nerves. There was a gleam of excitement in his eyes.

As they neared the bar, de Silva noticed that the glass at the man's elbow was empty, but his left hand was around the neck of a bottle of whisky. Unsteadily, he lifted it and tried to refill the glass, but instead, the whisky slopped onto the bar and began to drip over the edge. De Silva heard a mumbled curse and frowned. What was the accent the man spoke with? Had he got the wrong person?

Letting go of the bottle, which promptly rolled off the bar and smashed on the floor, the man lurched from his stool, ending up wedged between it and the front of the bar. The stool toppled and he struggled to get to his feet but fell again. His neighbour swore and pushed him away. Two barmen left what they were doing and hurried round. One ducked to avoid the punch the drunk threw at him, then they both grabbed him under the armpits. Hoisting him up, they dragged him to de Silva and Prasanna and deposited him at their feet. As they did so, de Silva saw his face. He wasn't Jack Harvey.

'Have you come to arrest him, sahib?' asked one of the men.

'He has not paid his bill,' the other chimed in. 'And getting dead drunk like this is bad for business.'

De Silva glanced around the room. It was hard to imagine anything that would lower the tone of the establishment, but he supposed the owners might have a point. He tossed a few annas onto the counter. 'That's all you're getting and be thankful for it. If I hadn't been here, I expect you would have thrown him out without paying. Next time, don't let him have so much whisky.'

One of the barmen scowled. Grumbling, both of them retreated behind the bar. The room had gone silent again; no one moved as they half carried, half walked the drunk out of the bar. In the street, he rallied briefly and tried to struggle, but then doubled over. Just in time, de Silva pushed him towards the gutter. A stream of vomit turned the black, evil-smelling water coursing along it to a greasy yellow.

When the bout was over, the man gasped for breath. 'You've nothing on me,' he mumbled. 'I've done nothing wrong.'

'Then you have nothing to fear, sir. But I suggest that a night in the police station to sleep off the alcohol is best for you.'

CHAPTER 14

Safely back at the police station, de Silva consoled himself that at least he didn't have to face Prasanna's wife, Kuveni, and tell her that her husband had been beaten up in Mackenzie Road; to say nothing of what Jane would have said if their escapade had gone awry. As it was, they had returned in one piece, even if they'd come back with the wrong man.

He turned his attention to the problem of the drunk sleeping it off in the cell. Prasanna had done enough today. It wouldn't be fair to leave him to guard the man all night. Nadar's little boy's birthday celebrations must be over by now.

'Go and find Constable Nadar,' he said to Prasanna. 'Tell him he's to report back for duty. When you've done that, you may go home.'

'Thank you, sir.' Prasanna hurried away.

While he waited for Nadar to arrive, de Silva went to check on the drunk. Curled up fast asleep like a small child, he looked harmless. In the morning, when he had sobered up, he would give him a stern warning not to behave in such a foolish fashion again.

He wondered what Jack Harvey was doing. Maybe he was back at the Harveys' bungalow by now. His brow furrowed at the thought of Elizabeth Harvey and Peter Hancock. They had both led him down the wrong path. Was that an honest mistake or had they tried to mislead him deliberately? If the latter, he had let them dupe him into wasting valuable time. He scratched his head. Where to go from here?

Unless any of their servants were prepared to talk freely, he had no idea how he was going to find out whether the alibis Mark Brodie and David Llewellyn had given each other were genuine. Unfortunately, most servants didn't want to jeopardise their jobs, so they feigned ignorance, or it might be genuine. He had a similar problem with Tom Duncan. At the moment, he had only his wife's evidence for the time he left home.

He wrote down Jack's name in his notebook and under-lined it. The evidence against him was more compelling. Why lie about the time he left the Blue Cat in Kandy if he had nothing to hide?

* * *

'I agree things look bad for Jack Harvey,' said Jane with a sigh when de Silva had finished recounting the day's events.

'I'm afraid they do.'

'I wonder who your drunk in the cells is.'

De Silva shrugged. 'That's the least of my worries. Probably someone who's had a row with his wife.'

'Oh, I hope it's not that. The poor lady will be frantic with worry if he doesn't come home. Are you sure there was nothing on him to identify him?'

'Quite sure.'

Savouring a mouthful of his whisky and soda, de Silva surveyed the darkened garden. Since dinner, the air had cooled, dropping a little moisture. A sliver of moon, lying on its back like a shallow bowl, hung above the trees; stars glittered in the ebony sky. He reminded himself that before the murders intervened on Friday – it seemed much longer than three days ago – he and Jane had planned a relaxing weekend, starting with a trip to the cinema.

'Police work is always unpredictable, isn't it,' said Jane as if she had read his thoughts. Sometimes, he thought that she did.

'I'm sorry it spoiled our weekend.'

'Oh, never mind. We shouldn't feel sorry for ourselves when poor Elizabeth Harvey has so much to grieve over.' She frowned. 'Particularly if it turns out to be true that her stepson is the one responsible.' She rested her chin on her hand. 'It does seem strange though.'

'How do you mean?'

'From what you've said, in the fullness of time, Jack would have inherited his grandfather's business. If he murdered him, that won't be the case. He would have given up a lot out of sheer impatience. And if they'd had an argument, wouldn't it be more likely he'd strike in the heat of the moment, rather than waiting until the next day and following his grandfather up to the golf course? Not to mention killing the caddy, who had done him no harm at all. If he acted impulsively on the one hand, storming off because of the argument, but with cold-blooded calculation on the other, it shows a considerable contradiction in his character.'

De Silva mulled her words over. 'It's a good point,' he said at last. 'But it still doesn't explain why he lied about where he was at the time Harvey and the caddy were killed. I agree that psychology has a part to play in solving a crime, but facts cannot be overruled.'

He swallowed the last of his whisky and stretched. 'Shall we have some music? I'd be glad of something to take my mind off the subject of murder for a while.'

'What a good idea.'

'What would you like to listen to?'

'You choose.'

In the drawing room, he flipped open the record case by the gramophone and looked through the contents. 'How about Beethoven?' he called out.

'That would be lovely.'

Soon, the opening bars of *The Moonlight Sonata* drifted out to the verandah.

CHAPTER 15

'Jack Harvey is here, sir,' Nadar whispered urgently.

'What do you mean, he's here? Has he come to give himself up?'

It was early the next morning, and de Silva and Jane were finishing breakfast when the telephone call came.

'No, sir,' Nadar went on. 'The gentleman who spent the night in the cells is a friend of his. I let him make one telephone call this morning when he woke up. It was Mr Harvey that he telephoned.'

'Do you have any idea where Harvey was when this fellow called him?'

'At the Harveys' plantation, sir. I had to look the number up for his friend.'

De Silva put a hand to his forehead and sighed deeply. The gods moved in a mysterious way. 'I'll be with you as fast as I can. Do whatever you have to. Just keep Harvey there.'

'Yes, sir.' De Silva heard a chuckle. 'I haven't taken the gentleman's statement yet. I will write very slowly.'

Back at the breakfast table, Jane was pouring herself another cup of tea. 'You look pleased, dear. Has something happened?'

'Jack Harvey's at the police station.'

'Goodness. Does he know you were looking for him?'

'I don't think so. As luck would have it, he happens to be a friend of that drunkard we pulled in yesterday evening.

He's going to get a nasty shock. He'll be expecting nothing more than to pay the fine and take his friend away. Nadar is going to keep him busy until I arrive. I'd better get straight off though. I'm not sure I should rely on my constable's inventiveness for too long.'

* * *

Jack Harvey was pacing up and down the public room at the station. He turned and glowered at de Silva when he came in.

'It's about time,' he said irritably. 'When I was dragged out of bed by my friend and asked for my help, I didn't expect to spend half the morning here. If there's a fine to pay, just tell me how much it is so we can settle and be on our way.' He scowled. 'It's a poor show if a fellow can't drown his sorrows without having to spend a night in the cells.'

'All in good time, sir. But first, I'm glad to see you here.'

Jack frowned. 'Why? Do you have some news about my grandfather? Have you found out who killed him?' He looked at de Silva with narrowed eyes. 'What's going on? As his grandson, I have a right to know.'

Edging across so that his back was to the door in case he needed to stop Jack Harvey escaping, de Silva drew a deep breath. 'At what time did you leave the Blue Cat club on Thursday night, sir?'

'What is this? I've already told you that I slept the night there.'

'Are you sure of that? Is it possible that you went on somewhere else and forgot to mention it?'

A sour note crept into Jack's voice. 'If you're implying that I was too drunk to know where I was, Inspector, I assure you, you're wrong. Now, shall we get back to the matter in hand?'

'Not yet, sir. I have to inform you that your story has been denied by the manager of the club. He says that you left there by eleven o'clock. Where did you go on to?'

Jack flushed. 'What a load of rot! I've no idea why the wretched fellow should lie, but when I get to the bottom of it—'

'That is something that I'm as keen to do as you are, sir. But for the moment, I must ask you not to leave Nuala.'

'Are you telling me what to do, Inspector? You're trying my patience.'

'I'm asking you, sir.'

'And what if I refuse?'

'Then I'm afraid you would leave me no alternative but to place you under arrest.'

CHAPTER 16

'Was he there?' asked Jane when they met in the hallway at Sunnybank.

'Yes. Nadar did a good job. But unfortunately, things didn't go all that smoothly afterwards.'

'Oh dear. I suppose it was only to be expected. Where is he now?'

'At the Residence. Archie was most insistent he be kept there rather than in the cells at the station.'

That was an edited version of the situation; to protect Jane's peace of mind, he didn't plan to go into too much detail. He'd actually had a very stormy conversation with Archie Clutterbuck, and it had been quite a while before the temperature lowered. It had been obvious that Archie would take a lot more convincing that Jack was guilty. Hard to know how much of his bad temper was attributable to genuine doubt and how much to the strain of the American ambassador's prolonged visit.

'Isn't having him at the Residence rather awkward with the American ambassador's party staying?'

'Apparently not. I suppose the Residence is big enough for the arrangement to be discreet.'

'What happens next?'

'He has the right to have his solicitor with him when he's questioned.'

'Who do you think he'll want?'

De Silva shrugged. 'Tom Duncan was his grandfather's solicitor. Jack may call on him.'

'I see him and his wife at church sometimes. Poor Ella Duncan, it's a shame that she always looks so unhappy. I do hope he's not unkind to her.'

De Silva wasn't inclined to concern himself with Mrs Duncan and her marriage difficulties, especially today, but he thought briefly back to his visit to the Duncans' home. He recalled her speaking warmly of the pleasure she derived from her Indian rug and making a point of it being her own, not something her husband had brought to their marriage. Perhaps one might read something into that.

'Has anyone told Elizabeth Harvey yet?' asked Jane.

'Archie's determined to do that himself. I think he wants to underplay the situation.'

'How will he do that?'

'I don't know. It's up to him. But on one level, I would have preferred to tell her myself.'

'To see her reaction, you mean?'

'Yes. It might be revealing. As it is, unless he relents and agrees to my being there, I shall have to rely on Archie.'

'Try not to be too cross, dear.'

'Cross? Who says I'm cross?'

'I hear it in your voice.'

'Just a bit, I suppose,' he grumbled.

'Perhaps a stroll around the garden would help. Lunch won't be ready for an hour.'

De Silva sighed. 'I'll try it.'

As he passed the frangipani tree, the sweet scent wafted towards him. Ordinarily, he would have been tempted to sit down on the bench nearby and enjoy it, but today he needed something more vigorous to work off the knot of irritation in his stomach.

In the vegetable garden, he took a spade from the shed and went over to a bare patch of earth. Onions had been growing there a few weeks ago, but they were all harvested now and hanging, neatly tied, in the cool larder behind the kitchen, waiting to be transformed into the basis for curries and stews. Usually, Anif, the gardener, prepared the bed for whatever would be planted next. Today, however, digging would provide a practical solution to some much-needed therapy.

The spade sliced into the dark, friable soil with satisfying ease. He turned the first load over then made another cut. A rhythm established, he let his mind drift. Slowly, Archie's irascible tones faded. The old chap would come around eventually; he always did. And if Jack's arrest had been a miscalculation, well then, he, de Silva, might have to eat – what was the English expression – humble pie? Yes, that was the one. But if he had to do so, he only intended to eat a very small portion. The more he thought about it, the more he decided that his action had been entirely justified.

He lifted a final load of soil, dumped it down and went back to the shed. When he had wiped the spade clean with the rag hung on a peg near the door for the purpose, he put the spade back in its place. Best to let Jane think he'd been enjoying a gentle stroll. She would tell him off for working in the heat, and his good clothes. He brushed a smattering of soil from the bottom of one trouser leg and went indoors.

'Archie called while you were outside, dear,' said Jane as he came into the drawing room.

Damn, he had missed him.

'He told me not to bother to call you in.'

'Was there a message?'

'Yes. Jack wants Tom Duncan with him when he's questioned. The meeting is set for tomorrow morning at ten o'clock. Archie wants you there.'

Well, that was something. At least he wasn't being completely sidelined.

'Aren't you glad?'

'I'm not sure yet. I'll decide that when I know what part Archie wants me to play.'

CHAPTER 17

The Residence's elegant white façade gleamed in the sunshine as the Morris cruised up the drive the following morning. At least half a dozen gardeners were at work hoeing flowerbeds and raking up the debris that had fallen from a grove of oleanders that grew to the right-hand side of the house. De Silva usually stopped to admire the glossy, dark green leaves and showy, pink flowers but right now, he was too preoccupied to pay them any attention.

Following the servant who answered the door along the cool passage to Archie's study, he steeled himself to maintain his dignity. At their first meeting, Tom Duncan had been perfectly civil, but he was in a different role now; his duty was to challenge the allegation against his client.

Both of them were already in the study with Archie when de Silva came in. At the sight of him, a resentful expression came over Jack Harvey's face. Tom Duncan's expression was impassive – the unruffled gaze of the lion before it pounces, thought de Silva.

Looking solemn, Archie stood up behind his desk. He nodded. 'Ah, you've joined us.'

De Silva hadn't been aware he was late: in fact, the reverse. He sensed that the assistant government agent was ill at ease. Perhaps the presence of the lawyer was making him uncomfortable. De Silva had taken the precaution of having a word with Inspector Singh, his counterpart at

Hatton, before coming up to the Residence. Singh had come across Tom Duncan on several occasions.

'I don't envy you having to deal with him,' Singh had said in his deep, rumbling voice. 'On the surface, he seems a reasonable man, but underneath, he's a bully. He treats the Ceylonese like dirt and is as wily as a crocodile, and as tenacious. He'll fight you every inch of the way.'

'I suppose it's right he should when his client's life is at stake.'

Singh had laughed at that. 'It would make no difference if his client had merely been accused of pilfering a bunch of bananas from a neighbour's tree.'

'Thank you for the warning. What's this about him mistreating people?'

'Well,' said Singh, 'for example, we have a couple of highly respected local lawyers practising here in Hatton, whom I know socially. They tell me that in business meetings, Duncan behaves towards them with little more than contempt. One of them used the British expression, "he speaks to me as though I was something to be scraped off the sole of his shoe". Apparently, it's as though anyone who isn't British, isn't worth caring about.'

'Curious,' said de Silva. 'I saw nothing of that when I interviewed him at home.' Maybe there was more to Duncan than he'd thought. 'You've been a great help, my friend. Many thanks.'

'My pleasure. Good luck.'

De Silva put the conversation to the back of his mind and readied himself for what lay ahead. Archie cleared his throat. 'You'd better kick off, de Silva. Tell us again what the manager of this club said to you.'

Inwardly, de Silva groaned. Immediately, the way Archie framed the question exposed a major weakness in his case. What on earth made his boss assume he'd had time to go down to Kandy himself? He would have needed the speed of a leopard to fit in a trip since they last spoke. If Duncan didn't pounce on the fact that he hadn't paid a visit to the club himself, but was relying on information from the Kandy police, he'd be very surprised. Perhaps unwittingly, Jack had made a very good move when he forced his hand. If Jack had undertaken not to leave Nuala until further notice, it would have been unnecessary to arrest him. There would have been time for de Silva to go down to Kandy himself and check the club manager's story.

'Yes, Inspector,' said Tom Duncan smoothly. 'My client and I are very interested in hearing what you have to say.' He raised an eyebrow and turned slightly in his chair so that his next remark was addressed more to Archie than to de Silva. 'You may not be surprised to hear that my client was profoundly shocked by the allegation made against him. Coming at a time when he's struggling to come to terms with his grief over the death of his grandfather, the impact is particularly acute. He regrets that he spoke hotly to the inspector – some might say it was unfortunate that his reaction was uncooperative – but I hope that in the circumstances, it is all too easy to understand. Isn't that right,' he paused, and then added pointedly, 'Inspector?'

'Indeed,' growled Archie, at least saving de Silva the need to respond to the obvious and unnecessary jibe. 'Well, de Silva. Let's have the answer. What did this fellow have to say to you?'

De Silva hesitated, but there was no use prevaricating. 'There has been no time to go down to Kandy myself, sir. The information comes from the Kandy police.' As Archie ought to know. Was this ambassadorial visit putting him completely off his stroke, or was he right that Duncan made Archie uncomfortable?

Archie frowned. 'So, you still haven't visited the club in person.'

Tom Duncan's eyes narrowed. 'Hearsay. Not the most

reliable type of evidence, wouldn't you agree, gentlemen? Certainly wouldn't wash in a court of law. Who did you pass the job to in Kandy, Inspector?' Again there had been a slight delay before Duncan acknowledged de Silva's rank.

Now Duncan made him sound lazy as well as incompetent.

'Inspector Jayaratne.'

'Did he go to the club himself?'

De Silva squirmed. 'I believe he sent one of his officers.'

Permitting himself a slight smile, Duncan nodded. 'One of his "officers". I see.' A note of sarcasm crept into his voice. 'And did you receive the information from this "officer", or from Jayaratne himself?'

A lead weight settled in de Silva's stomach. 'It was relayed to me by another member of staff at Kandy.'

Duncan rolled his eyes, raised his hands and shrugged. 'Maybe not even an "officer" then. Who knows, maybe somebody who can barely understand the King's English? A long chain of, if I may be forgiven, "Chinese whispers"? I rest my case.'

Jack, who had been silent since he and Duncan arrived, raised his head. 'The owner of the roadhouse where I stopped to eat on the way back from Kandy will vouch for the fact that I was there at around two. It's an hour's drive at least from there back to Nuala. You said my grandfather was killed in the morning.'

Duncan put a hand on his arm. 'In the circumstances, Jack, I don't think we need to go into that.' He turned to Archie. 'Clutterbuck, I trust you'll agree with me that the inspector's case against my client is flimsy in the extreme. With respect, I'm surprised it was allowed to go this far. I'd be obliged if you would confirm he's now free to come and go as he pleases.'

Archie had flushed slightly. 'Have you anything to say about that, de Silva?'

Glumly, de Silva shook his head. 'No, sir.'

There was a long pause, broken by Archie.

'You've made your point, Duncan. Harvey, you're free to go.' As the two men rose to their feet, he gestured to de Silva. 'No need for you to leave. I'd like a word.'

* * *

'Dashed awkward,' growled Archie when the door had closed behind Tom Duncan and Jack Harvey.

'I'm sorry, sir. At the time, arresting Harvey seemed the only way forward.'

Rather to de Silva's surprise, Archie waved the apology away. 'No need for that. I appreciate you were backed into a corner.'

De Silva was puzzled. What had made Archie think that?

'Young Frobisher filled me in.' This was even more puzzling. De Silva hadn't spoken to Charlie Frobisher since Jack Harvey's arrest.

'Frobisher's had a few conversations with young Harvey up at the Residence and he thinks we can't assume he's telling the truth. I'm not sure I would have made the arrest myself, but Frobisher convinced me that since Harvey refused to cooperate, it's arguable you did the right thing.'

Silently, de Silva blessed Charlie Frobisher. The young man was a very welcome ally.

'All the same,' Archie went on. 'We have a problem. If Harvey's our man, you'll need to find some powerful evidence if we're to arrest him again.' Archie gave de Silva a hard look. 'I don't intend to give Duncan the chance to humiliate us a second time. Never liked the fellow much,' he added reflectively. 'Far too sure of his own opinions for my taste. Not a team player, and I don't care for his tone.'

Some might say that, on occasion, Archie was pretty fond of his own opinions too, thought de Silva, then felt guilty. Today, he couldn't fault the assistant government agent on supportiveness, despite the fact that the case wasn't going well.

Archie reached for the cigarette box on his desk and opened it. De Silva was almost tempted to accept one if he was offered it, but Archie just took one for himself and lit up.

'The question is,' he said, shaking out the match, 'what do we do next?'

Without waiting for an answer, he went on. 'Well, there's one loophole we can plug. Get down to that club in Kandy and make the manager repeat his story. Unfortunately, it will probably be as much use as flogging a dead horse and we won't be able to disprove Jack Harvey's alibi, but I come across Inspector Jayaratne sometimes when I go down to do my bit at the courts there. Pompous idiot. I wouldn't rely on him to find a lost dog.'

Although de Silva echoed Archie's views, he was slightly nettled by the implication that he shouldn't have trusted Jayaratne either.

'I'd like to be more involved, but this American party seems to have taken root. Dashed inconvenient. Having to get trussed up in black tie and starched collars every night and sit through formal dinners isn't my idea of a good time.' Archie rubbed his nose with a stubby forefinger. 'Still, William Petrie expects my wife and me to do our duty. I just hope some good comes of it. Changing the subject, what about Hancock, Harvey's manager? Have you spoken to him?'

'I have, sir.'

'Did he shed any light?'

De Silva shook his head.

'Might he be our man? I understand he's worked for

Harvey for many years. He must be a tough nut to have coped with Harvey for as long as he has, but every man has his breaking point.'

'I think not, sir. He claims he was at the plantation all day meeting with an agent up from Colombo then dealing with a shipment of tea that was due to go down to an export firm there by the end of that day. He gave me the numbers of the companies and the names of the people he deals with. I still need to check with them, but I don't expect his alibi to be false.' De Silva winced. Alibis were a painful subject at the moment.

With a smile that was surprisingly sympathetic, Archie nodded. 'Do so,' he said kindly. 'No more slipups, eh?'

CHAPTER 18

Before he returned to Sunnybank for lunch, de Silva went to the police station. He would enjoy his meal more if he didn't have the job of checking Hancock's alibis on his conscience.

At the first company in Colombo Hancock had given him the name of, the receptionist tried to find the man with whom he wanted to speak, but after several attempts to track him down, she suggested de Silva call back. He had no better luck finding out whether the shipment Hancock mentioned had been expected at the right time. Various fruitless conversations later, he gave up.

After lunch, he decided to allow himself a brief nap before going back to the police station to try again. He was disturbed by the sound of the telephone ringing. Scowling, he hoped it wasn't Archie checking up on him. He went inside but found it was only the vicar's wife wanting to talk to Jane about a forthcoming meeting of school governors.

'Are you feeling better, dear?' she asked, when the call ended.

'To tell the truth, not much.'

'But you said Archie was surprisingly sympathetic.'

'He was, mainly thanks to Charlie Frobisher. I hope I have the opportunity to express my gratitude to that young man soon. But I saw Archie was embarrassed. He told me he doesn't like Duncan much. And today I saw a side to Duncan I hadn't seen when I interviewed him. It was obviously distasteful that he won the day. And so easily.'

He sighed. 'I even let Jack Harvey off on a point he made about the roadside place where he stopped for lunch being able to vouch for the time he was there. He said it was an hour's drive from there to Nuala, but would they have known for sure which way he was going? He might have been coming from the golf course, not returning to town. If Duncan hadn't taken control of the meeting as he did—'

'Dear, I think you should forget about Mr Duncan. Let him enjoy his little triumph. It probably won't be for long.'

De Silva smiled wryly. 'Not such a little triumph, my love. And if Jack Harvey is the guilty party, I'm fresh out of ideas for how I'm going to catch him out.'

'Oh, something will come up. You'll see.'

'I hope you're right.'

He yawned. 'I suppose I'd better be getting back to the station.'

Once again, the telephone rang. 'Maybe this will be your answer already,' said Jane cheerfully.

'I doubt that.' He picked up the receiver. It was Charlie Frobisher calling from the Residence. Good; if nothing else, here was his opportunity to thank him for his help.

'Mr Frobisher! Good afternoon to you. I understand I have you to thank for getting me out of an awkward situation.'

'Don't mention it. Jack Harvey can be a hothead at the best of times. I felt it was very unfair that you should be the one to suffer for it.'

'I'm not sure his solicitor would agree with your view,' de Silva said dryly.

Frobisher laughed. 'It would do Duncan no harm to be taken down a peg or two. In any case, that's not the real reason for my call. The boss is happy to do without me for a couple of days if I can be of any use to you. Does anything come to mind?'

De Silva ran over the outstanding issues he hadn't resolved yet. If verifying Peter Hancock's alibis was going to be a problem at a distance, he might have to go down to Colombo. That would take up the best part of two days. Frobisher, on the other hand, might be able to arrange for one of the officials down there to pay a visit to the companies.

When he explained the situation, Frobisher volunteered immediately to help.

'The details are at the station. I'll send them over this afternoon.' De Silva reached for the pen and paper beside the telephone and made a note.

'That sounded like good news,' said Jane when he rang off.

'Yes. Archie's letting Charlie Frobisher off his duties for a few days so that he can give me a hand. I think he'll have more luck checking out Peter Hancock's alibi than I did this morning.'

'Good. That can be one thing off your mind. And I imagine Frobisher's help is more welcome than Archie's at present,' she added.

De Silva smiled ruefully. 'That's true, but to be fair, it doesn't sound like he's having an easy time of it. The American ambassador's party is still at the Residence, and I think Archie will be relieved when the visit's over. He's already told me he's not fond of all the formality involved.'

Jane smiled. 'I gather from Florence that even she's beginning to find it rather a strain. I hope some good comes of it in the end with some new trade deals.'

CHAPTER 19

'What are you doing today?' de Silva asked Jane the following morning.

'It's my turn to do the church flowers. Emerald Watson is collecting me. She's coming to help.'

A stab of alarm went through de Silva. Emerald's last attempt at driving a few years ago had been more courageous than skilled. 'Has she learnt to drive now?' he asked cautiously.

'Oh, no. The Applebys' driver is bringing her. Although she tells me that David Hebden has promised to teach her. She may even get a little car of her own.' Jane looked pensive. 'I've been wondering whether I might like to learn to drive myself. What do you think?'

She paused, then burst out laughing. 'I wish you could see the look on your face, dear. I'm only teasing, of course. I wouldn't dream of driving your beloved Morris. Now, you must be off, and I must get ready. I already have the greenery I plan to use, and Emerald is bringing some extra bits and pieces, but I need Anif to bring me the flowers you agreed we may take from the garden.'

He kissed her on the cheek. 'Enjoy your morning. Now I have Charlie Frobisher checking on Mr Hancock's story, I'll go down to Kandy to keep Archie happy, but I hope not to be too late home.'

Looking fresh and pretty in a red-and-white polka dot dress with the collar and sleeves trimmed in white, Emerald Watson arrived to collect Jane an hour later. 'Good morning,' she said smiling. She touched the petals of one of the flowers in the basket Jane had ready to take up to the church. 'How lovely. Inspector de Silva is so clever to grow such beautiful ones.'

Jane laughed. 'I think our gardener, Anif, has something to do with it, but Shanti certainly likes to fuss over them when he has time.'

The drive to the church didn't take long. Inside, the Applebys' servant, who had accompanied them, carried their flowers and greenery through to the little room set aside for flower arranging behind the vestry. Emerald told him to return for them later.

Jane took a pair of gardening gloves out of her basket. She studied the pedestals on either side of the altar steps. 'These orchids looked so pretty on Sunday. I think they're from one of the greenhouses at the Residence. What a pity they don't last, but I think we can reuse some of the greenery.'

As they worked on their new arrangements in the back room, they chatted amicably. 'I saw Ella Duncan in town the other day,' remarked Emerald after a while. 'When I mentioned we were doing the flowers today, she said she might come down to help us. I offered to give her a lift if she decided to come, but since then, I've heard nothing from her. It's strange. At the time, she appeared very eager – as if it was going to be a relief.'

'Never mind. It was kind of her, but I think we'll manage.'

'I hope everything's alright,' mused Emerald. 'She seemed rather low, but then she often does. I've wondered whether she's happy with her life, but it's hard to judge. I don't know her well, and as she doesn't invite friendship, I doubt I ever will.'

Jane nodded. 'I've wondered the same myself. But as you say, she's not easy to get to know. Her husband seems successful, so I doubt she lacks for much, but that isn't always enough. From the little I have heard he doesn't sound like he'd be the most considerate of husbands.'

She stood back to survey her handiwork. 'I think that's enough. I'll take this one through.'

'I'll be done soon.'

Carefully, Jane carried her arrangement into the church. As she passed the altar, the sound of the west door opening echoed down the nave. Perhaps it was Ella Duncan joining them after all. But it was only Reverend Peters, with his bumbling manner and the faint smell of peppermints that always hung about him. He took the vase of flowers from her and placed it on the pedestal.

'Charming, charming,' he murmured. 'We're lucky to have so many talented ladies to give their time to the church.'

'Oh, we do enjoy it,' said Jane with a smile.

He glanced over her shoulder. 'And Miss Watson as well. Good morning to you. I'm glad we met. You and Doctor Hebden are most welcome to visit us at the vicarage to discuss your nuptials. Just name a time.'

'How kind of you, but we thought we should let a decent interval pass after poor Mr Harvey's sudden death, at least until after the funeral.' It was still not common knowledge how Harvey had died.

The vicar pushed his spectacles down his beaky nose and looked absently over the top of them. 'Ah yes, a sad business.' He shook his head. 'The Lord moves in mysterious ways. None of us knows when we'll be called. I visited his widow, but I fear my words may not have provided her with much consolation.'

'Oh, I'm sure she appreciated your visit,' said Jane brightly, although privately she suspected that Reverend Peters' well-meaning vagaries would have irritated Elizabeth Harvey more than they consoled her. Still, he was a good man.

'Well, I mustn't keep you, ladies. I just came to ... er...'

There was a long pause. To break it, they said their goodbyes and left the vicar to wander in the direction of the vestry.

'Probably he came to get out from under his wife's feet,' said Emerald with a giggle as she and Jane went out through the west door. In the churchyard, she shaded her eyes against the brightness of the sun. 'I hope Raju's waiting with the car. We were much quicker than I thought we'd be.' She glanced around. 'Ah, good, there he is.'

Soon, they were ensconced in the Applebys' comfortable Rover, nudging through the town traffic on their way to Sunnybank. Emerald stopped in the middle of what she was saying. 'Oh look, isn't that Ella Duncan now? Over there in that rickshaw.'

Jane followed her pointing finger. 'Why yes, it is. She may be on her way to the church. Perhaps we should have waited a little longer.'

Emerald frowned. 'The Applebys have a lunch party, and I promised to be there.'

'Oh, then never mind. I'm sure Reverend Peters will explain. After all, Ella never telephoned you to say she was definitely coming.'

The Rover speeded up a little as the driver passed a bullock cart that had been lumbering along in front of them for several minutes.

Back at Sunnybank, Jane unpinned her hat and went to the flower room to put away her basket and secateurs. Briefly, she thought once again of Ella Duncan. Would it be a kindness to pay her a visit? She closed the cupboard and as she did so, her eye fell on the golf club cover de Silva had brought home. It should have been thrown away. She picked it up and paused. Perhaps she'd wait and have one last try after lunch at deciphering the marks inside.

* * *

'I'm glad we didn't give up,' she said, turning the edge of the lining inside out and showing it to de Silva.

'You mean, you didn't,' he said with a smile. It was good that something positive had emerged from the day. His plan to go down to Kandy had been thwarted by an overturned truck that had closed the road about thirty miles from Nuala. It was too late to take a train, so he had returned to the station with nothing to show for his trouble. Hopefully, Archie wouldn't ask about the visit again too soon, even if it was just a loose end to be tied up.

'Let me get the magnifying glass again,' Jane went on, 'and I'll show you what I mean.'

She returned a moment later with the glass and held it and the cover out to him. He examined the place she indicated.

'Do you see? If you try to hold the chewed threads more together – yes, like that – there are definitely two letters there, even though the rest is missing or impossible to make out. I think one of them is an "H", and after that bit that's been torn away, a "V".'

She was right. Through the glass, it was evident there was something and it did look like an "H" and a "V".

'If you ask to see the membership list, it would tell us how many members of the club have the letters "H" and "V" in their names.'

'Good idea. Although without a "J", it doesn't prove that this belongs to Jack Harvey rather than his grandfather.'

'Neither does it prove it doesn't. Anyway, didn't Charlie Frobisher tell you that all the covers he'd expect were on Bernard Harvey's clubs? If there are no other members whose names have an "H" and a "V" in them, might it be possible to have a look at Jack's to see if there's a club without its cover?'

De Silva peered closely at the exposed letters. 'It might. But I'll have to be careful how I approach it with Archie. He won't want to tangle with Tom Duncan again unless we're on very firm ground.'

'Does Archie know about this?' Jane indicated the cover.

'Not yet, but I'll ask Charlie Frobisher to mention it.'

'Then I'm sure he would arrange for you to have a look at the membership list.'

He smiled. 'It may lead us nowhere, I'm afraid.'

Jane shook her head reprovingly. 'But it may. No stone unturned, remember?'

De Silva laughed. 'Thank you for reminding me.'

He put the cover down. 'As it may be useful after all, we may as well try to preserve what's left of it. I think I'll make that telephone call to the Residence. If I can catch Charlie Frobisher, I'll ask him to talk Archie.'

'All done,' he said when he returned.

'Then sit down and have your coffee.'

She held out a plate. 'Try one of these cinnamon biscuits. I showed cook how to make them this afternoon.'

De Silva took a crumbly, sweet bite. 'Delicious.'

They drank their coffee and afterwards, Jane carried on with a new detective novel she had taken out from the library. De Silva's mind was too full to read. There was still Elizabeth Harvey's alibi for the time before she lunched at the Crown Hotel to check, and that wretched visit to the Blue Cat club in Kandy to make. He hoped he had better luck next time. Maybe he would take the train instead of driving.

He sighed. Neither avenue struck him as promising.

Why would the manager at the Blue Cat invent a false story? In other circumstances, it would be a good outcome to have his main suspect confirmed, but here, it would probably lead to a battle with Archie. Saying he wanted stronger evidence was one thing, but how to find it another.

Jane closed her book.

'Any good?' he asked.

'Not a patch on Mrs Christie, but then few writers are. I'm sure I've read the same plot at least twice before.'

He grinned. 'You must be able to write the things yourself by now.'

'Hardly, dear. It would be far too time consuming. Anyway, I like books to be my relaxation, not hard work.'

Stretching, he yawned. 'I think I'll have an early night. It's been a long day.'

In the hall, he stopped to inhale the scent of the bowl of orchids on the side table. In the pale light filtering through from the drawing room, their petals loomed out of the shadows like miniature ghostly faces. Jane had planted them in her favourite bowl, a big-bellied, oval-shaped one, decorated with Chinese dragons and peonies. The orchids' stems nestled in damp, dark green moss.

The ring of the telephone, so close to his ear, startled him. He waited a moment to collect himself, then picked up the receiver.

'De Silva here.'

It was Charlie Frobisher again. 'Sorry to disturb you at this hour. I've been stuck in a reception most of the evening. This afternoon, I had it confirmed that Peter Hancock's alibi checks out, but perhaps more importantly, I thought you'd like to know that I mentioned this cover to the boss. He'd like you to come up to the golf club tomorrow morning.'

'May I ask why?'

'Mark Brodie was at the reception. Apparently, the boss asked his opinion about this cover. With great respect to

Mrs de Silva, Brodie thought it was a wild goose chase. He hasn't dismissed the theory that the murders are the result of a bungled robbery by a person, or persons, unknown who ran off empty-handed. He's also suggesting there might be political motives behind all this. Naturally, that's a matter of great concern to the boss. Well, to us all.'

De Silva thought of his discussion with Jane. Were these crimes the start of a much greater problem? If so, even she might be in danger. An icy sensation pricked his spine. Like anyone who loved their country, he desired its independence, but not at any price.

He realised that Frobisher wasn't speaking. 'Of course,' he said quickly.

There was a chuckle at the other end of the line. 'Thank you. Anyway,' Frobisher went on, 'he's very keen to clear Jack's name of even the slightest vestige of suspicion. He's suggested that we meet him up at the club at six thirty tomorrow morning. He has a pass key, so we'll be able to check Jack's locker without causing comment. None of the members will be around at that hour. Brodie says Jack always leaves his bag in his locker. If the covers on his clubs are all as they should be, that will be the end of the matter as far as Archie's concerned.'

When Frobisher had rung off, de Silva put down the receiver and remained by the telephone for a while, deep in thought. On one level, he shouldn't resent Mark Brodie for being keen to help, but on another, it was irksome. He disliked the fact that Brodie was discussing the case with Archie behind his, de Silva's back, and probably not for the first time. He appeared to be one of those people with a high opinion of themselves who loved to meddle. He'd clearly relished needling poor old David Hebden over Emerald Watson. De Silva suspected he would enjoy imposing such an inconveniently early meeting on tomorrow's participants too. No, it was wrong to be ungenerous.

Brodie was probably motivated by genuine concern for Jack Harvey. No point letting this latest development ruin his early night. He'd need his wits about him in the morning.

CHAPTER 20

Jane woke him before dawn. He groaned but resisted the urge to roll over and go back to sleep. In the bathroom, he switched on the light and shuddered at the bleary-eyed creature who stared back at him from the mirror above the basin. The early night hadn't done as much good as he'd hoped, but when he'd splashed his face with cold water, he felt a little better. Twenty minutes later, washed, shaved and dressed, he ate the toast and tea Jane had ordered for him before setting off for the golf club. As he drove, he was glad of the scarf and gloves he wore. He and Jane always disagreed on the subject of being cold, but her English tolerance of it was far higher than his.

By the time he reached the club, the sun was above the horizon. The early morning light softened the building's severe lines. Sun glinted on the windowpanes, and a light mist hung over the flowerbeds.

Charlie Frobisher's MG followed him into the parking area. De Silva was surprised to see Archie ease himself out of the passenger seat. He strode over to the Morris.

'Haven't had a ride like that in years. Takes me back to my younger days. Might pay for it later, though.' Archie rubbed his side. 'Right, shall we get this business over with? I'm looking forward to a good breakfast afterwards. The kitchen here turns out a very decent one. I usually indulge when there's an early match to play.'

Archie was taking a very light-hearted attitude to this, thought de Silva irritably. He bore Jack Harvey no ill-will, but it was tempting to hope there would be something that, at least for the moment, left the young man's innocence in doubt. It would be galling to be regarded as the pebble in the shoe who had inconvenienced everyone to no purpose.

A figure emerged from the clubhouse; de Silva recognised Mark Brodie.

Archie raise a hand in greeting. 'Good of you to meet us at this unearthly hour, old chap. Frobisher drove me over. Lucky fellow's still of an age when you jump out of bed all bright-eyed and bushy-tailed.'

A glance at Frobisher confirmed this was an apt description. He smiled and wished Brodie and de Silva a good morning. Increasingly, de Silva doubted it would be a good one for him.

Inside the clubhouse, following Brodie's lead, they trooped down a long corridor, its walls lined with prints of golfing cartoons, passing the committee room that de Silva remembered and several others. Across a small courtyard, there was another corridor, this time with no pictures on the walls.

Finally, Brodie stopped at a door. Pulling a bunch of keys from his pocket, he selected one and unlocked. 'We like to keep the locker rooms secured overnight.' He held up the bunch of keys by a small one. 'This is the pass key to all the lockers.' He went over to one of them. 'Well, gentlemen; the moment of truth. I'm confident all will be well.'

The locker door swung open to reveal a bag of clubs. Mark Brodie reached in and hauled it out. They all leant forward for a better look. After a few moments, Archie scowled. 'Well I'll be damned. You may have stumbled on something here, de Silva. There's a cover missing.'

* * *

The mood around the table in the committee room was sombre. Reaching for a bottle of brown sauce, Archie put a large dollop of the concoction on his plate then stabbed his fork into his egg. The yellow yolk, streaked with muddy brown sauce, oozed over his bacon.

'I'd never have believed it if I hadn't seen the evidence with my own eyes,' he said morosely.

'Neither would I.' Mark Brodie put down his cup of tea.

Archie eyed his own cup disapprovingly. De Silva suspected he was thinking it was a pity it was too early for something stronger.

Charlie Frobisher, who hadn't spoken since they sat down, polished off the last of a gargantuan helping of bacon and eggs.

'If I may say so, sir,' he said, looking in Archie's direction, 'I'm surprised Jack took the risk of bringing his bag back to the locker room. He might well have had time to clean his club out on the course, but he also had to hide the caddy's body, which would take time. I appreciate the course was closed until lunchtime, but there might easily have been people about.'

'Unlikely any members would have come in, but you're right,' Archie said. 'When he came back there might have been kitchen or bar staff about.' He turned to de Silva. 'What do you say about that?'

'It's a good point, sir. And if it was Jack Harvey, unless he managed to change his clothes, there must have been very visible blood on them after the attack, and he would have had to clean himself up as well.'

'We were all loath to believe ill of Jack,' said Brodie gloomily. 'But this throws a disturbing light on the matter. He'll need a very convincing explanation before we can eliminate him from our inquiries now.'

'Do you see much prospect of one being forthcoming?' asked Archie.

'I wouldn't like to predict either way.'

They fell silent as a steward came in to clear the plates, then returned with a fresh pot of tea, a rack of toast, and silver dishes of butter and marmalade. When he had left the room, Archie reached for a piece of toast and started to butter it. 'We'd better decide what to do. Anyone got any ideas about where we might find Jack?'

They all shook their heads.

'That's unfortunate.' Archie took a spoonful of marmalade and spread it over his piece of buttered toast. De Silva smelt the sharp scent of Seville oranges. 'You'd better get on with it, de Silva.'

A pity he'd been let go in the first place, but de Silva refrained from voicing his opinion. Archie looked very tired and irritable; allowances should be made. This protracted official visit to the Residence appeared to be taking a considerable toll. Nuala wasn't usually a hotbed of activity. His guess was that Archie's usual routine wasn't too taxing. The need to engage with important visitors for any length of time must be interfering with his golf and fishing to an unwelcome degree. Once it was all over, life would no doubt return to normal.

Archie finished his toast and dropped his crumpled napkin onto the table. He pushed back his chair.

'Well, gentlemen, I must be getting along. I'd like a progress report this evening. Get your men on the job, de Silva. I want Jack found, and quickly. Frobisher, I suggest you lend a hand.'

'Yes, sir.'

Feeling that Charlie Frobisher was his only real friend at the Residence, de Silva smiled. 'I would appreciate that.'

'And if you have any ideas, Brodie, don't hesitate to pass them on.'

Brodie nodded.

'Right, let's get to work, gentlemen.'

CHAPTER 21

Shortly after de Silva left for the golf club, the telephone rang at Sunnybank.

'I hope it's not too early to call?' It was Emerald Watson.

'Of course not. Shanti and I were up with the lark.'

'If you're not too busy today, would you like to come to Hatton with me? They have some new hats in at Bentley's, and I need something to match my going-away outfit.'

Jane thought of her plans to go over the minutes of the last meeting of the Parish Council, but there was no rush. She'd enjoy a day out with Emerald much more.

'I'd be delighted.'

'Shall I pick you up at ten?'

'Lovely.'

The road to Hatton took them through gentle hills cloaked with tea terraces.

'I don't think I'll ever get used to how beautiful it is up here,' said Emerald as they drove along. 'Even my father said the Hill Country was a match for the green hills of Ireland.'

'We're very lucky to live up here. I enjoyed my time in Colombo, but it was so noisy and dusty. In the hot season, the heat was sometimes unbearable. It took me a long time to get used to it. By the time the monsoon came, I was desperate for rain. When Shanti and I were first married, he used to tease me about my British hankering for wet weather.'

'It's supposed to be better for the complexion.'

'But not so good for rheumatism,' replied Jane with a smile.

They had reached the outskirts of Hatton, a mixture of comfortable bungalows set in well-watered gardens, and the smaller homes of the local people. The Applebys' driver slowed the car to negotiate rickshaws, goats, and pedestrians carrying bundles and baskets of goods. Cows ambled along the road, tossing their heads and flicking their tails to rid themselves of the flies that clustered around their faces. A water cart was laden with an excited cargo of children sitting astride it.

The centre of town was even busier. In the main square, food stalls were doing a brisk trade and a market was in full swing. The street where the British shops were situated, however, was much quieter. Emerald and Jane were the only customers in the hat shop. Emerald tried on several and finally chose two: a red cloche with a curled brim and grosgrain ribbon trim, and a straw boater trimmed with a pink silk rose. When she had paid for her purchases, they drove on to the hotel by the lake.

'I hope David likes them,' said Emerald as they sat in the dining room having a light lunch.

'I'm sure he will. They both suit you so well.'

'Are there any other shops you'd like to visit after lunch?'

Jane shook her head. 'No, I don't need anything today. I was wondering though if we might call on Ella Duncan on the way home. The Duncans live very close to the Hatton road.'

'What a good idea. We can apologise for not waiting for her at church.'

'Yes. And I've been thinking since then that I really ought to make more effort with her. I've only been to their house once, and it was quite some time ago, but I think I can remember the way.'

Lunch over, they set off in the direction of Nuala. The diversion to the Duncans' bungalow was a short one. Soon the car drew up at the gates where a guard waved them through. Jane gazed out of the window as they approached the bungalow. To her eyes, it lacked the elegant architecture of the Residence or the charm of Sunnybank, and she found the style of the garden, with its low box hedges and regimented flowerbeds, too formal for her taste.

The sound of the doorbell died away forlornly. 'Perhaps we should come back another time,' said Emerald when no one answered.

'Let's wait a while longer.'

At that moment, the door opened a crack, and a servant peered out. She was elderly and had a wary expression on her wrinkled face.

'Is the memsahib in?' asked Jane.

'Memsahib is resting.'

'Then we won't disturb her. Would you say Mrs de Silva and Miss Watson called? If she went to the church the other day, please tell her we were sorry to miss her.'

'We thought she must have changed her mind about coming, and we couldn't wait any longer,' Emerald added.

A voice called out from somewhere in the bungalow. With a muttered request for them to come inside, the woman opened the door wider, then gathering up the hem of her sari, she shuffled away in the direction the voice had come from.

Jane looked around the hall where two fat flies buzzed against a windowpane and a thirsty plant drooped in one corner. As far as she recalled, the hall's appearance hadn't changed much since her last visit. There were the same drab curtains, an overly carved console table, a rack for coats and hats, and a metal stand for umbrellas and walking sticks.

'The memsahib is coming,' said the old woman when she shuffled back. She beckoned them into the drawing room and left them there.

'What a dispiriting room,' whispered Emerald. 'It's a pity. The proportions are good. It could be made very nice.' She gestured to the taupe curtains and the olive-green sofas and chairs. 'Brighter colours would make such a difference. And the pictures—' She shuddered. 'So gloomy.' She glanced out of the window. 'But the view's lovely.'

'If I remember rightly, this room was decorated in the same way the last time I visited. Perhaps Ella Duncan isn't interested in interior decoration.'

'It might help if she was,' said Emerald firmly. 'This room would certainly depress me. Once David and I are married, I'm determined to make changes to his house as soon as possible. More comfortable furniture and pretty fabrics; that kind of thing. It's been a bachelor's abode far too long.'

Jane put a finger to her lips. 'I think she's coming,' she murmured.

'How nice to see you. It's kind of you to come all this way.' Ella Duncan's nervous expression belied the words.

'Not at all. We were passing and wanted to apologise if we missed you at church the other day.'

'Oh, I'm the one who should apologise. I was delayed and—' She paused then resumed hurriedly. 'Do take a seat. I've asked Nita to bring us some tea.'

'What a delightful view you have,' said Emerald as they sat down. 'If I lived here, I'd want to spend all my time enjoying it.'

With an absent air, almost as if she had never noticed it before, Ella Duncan turned her eyes to the view. 'I suppose it is pretty. Tom wanted us to live here. I'm used to it now, but I liked our old home in Hatton better.'

An awkward silence ensued, broken by the servant bringing the tea. As Ella Duncan poured, Jane noticed that the silver sugar bowl and tongs were slightly tarnished, and the rims of the rosebud-patterned cups and saucers had lost their gilt sheen. When she passed them their tea, Ella Duncan's hand was unsteady. Perhaps Emerald had been right after all, thought Jane; they shouldn't have waited. Rather than cheering Ella Duncan up, their visit seemed to make her anxious.

'We've been to Hatton this morning,' Emerald said brightly. 'Jane kindly kept me company. I wanted to choose a hat for my going-away outfit. In the end I bought two,' she added with a laugh. 'They had such pretty ones in Bentley's. You really should have a look.'

Silence descended again. 'Do you still go to Hatton to shop?' asked Jane to break it.

'Hardly ever.'

'Of course, the shops in Nuala have improved a great deal since we first came here. But Hatton has more choice, and it's not nearly as far as Colombo or Kandy.'

The silence returned.

'Do you play golf, Mrs Duncan?' asked Emerald, a faintly desperate note in her voice.

An unexpected flash of alarm passed over Ella Duncan's face, replaced by a blank expression. 'No. My husband enjoys it, but I don't think I should.'

'Perhaps you might try,' said Emerald encouragingly. 'David Hebden, my fiancé, is teaching me. I find it great fun.'

Ella Duncan shook her head. 'I doubt my husband wants to teach me,' she said flatly. She reached for the teapot. 'May I offer you more tea?' She reached out to take Jane's cup, and her sleeve slipped back a little. There was a bandage on her forearm.

'Oh dear, you've hurt yourself,' said Jane.

Quickly, Ella pulled down the sleeve. 'It's nothing. I was just picking roses for the house and caught my arm. Clumsy of me.'

'Goodness, how awkward that was,' said Emerald when, after more tea and another quarter of an hour of stilted conversation, they'd taken their leave. 'I wish she'd said it was a bad time to call. I felt we were intruding.' She frowned. 'Do you think she'd been drinking? There was a smell of gin.'

'Emerald!'

'Oh. I won't say anything. It's no business of mine if she has a drink in the afternoon. I expect she's bored stiff stuck away on her own in that place. She really ought to take up golf.'

'I'm afraid golf isn't the answer to everything, Emerald.' Jane sighed. 'But you're right; it was awkward. Perhaps the next time we see her she'll be feeling more sociable. Poor lady. Clearly something is making her unhappy.'

She wondered if Ella Duncan would ever confide what that was. As for the story about the roses, it didn't ring true. They had finished flowering weeks ago at Sunnybank, and she hadn't noticed any in flower in the Duncans' garden.

CHAPTER 22

If Jack had murdered his grandfather, why would he take the risk of returning his clubs to his locker afterwards? The question continued to puzzle de Silva as he left the clubhouse. Perhaps he'd simply thought there was little chance of being spotted. But if anyone had seen him, unless he'd managed to clean himself up and change his clothes, it would have been obvious that he'd been up to no good.

A voice behind him calling his name made him turn to see Charlie Frobisher. 'The boss wanted a word with Brodie,' he said. 'Can you spare a moment?'

'Of course.'

Frobisher pointed to a grove of palm trees beyond the parking area. 'If you don't mind, I'd rather stand in the shade. A bit more private too.'

Following him, de Silva wondered what was coming next.

'What's your opinion on this missing cover?' Frobisher asked when they reached the trees, disturbing a monitor lizard that rapidly disappeared into the undergrowth.

'I confess I'm perturbed. Why Jack would take the risk of bringing his clubs back to his locker and leaving the murder weapon there without its distinctive cover is a mystery. Surely he would have seen that the cover was gone and been worried it might be near his grandfather's body.'

'There's certainly no shortage of mystery in this whole

business. At least when we find Jack, Duncan won't be able to dismiss the case as easily as he did the first time. That should make Archie feel more comfortable.'

'I hope so.' And make me more comfortable too, thought de Silva.

'D'you know, de Silva, I can't help feeling there's something odd about Brodie in all of this.'

Certainly, Brodie had seemed very eager to search Jack's locker when Archie mentioned the club cover. Was it purely out of the desire to clear Jack's name or was there a different motive behind it? Something pricked de Silva's policeman's instinct. What about Brodie and Llewellyn's alibis? Unless Llewellyn's servants could be persuaded to talk freely, they only had each other to back them up. 'Are you thinking Brodie was a little too keen on getting involved?' he asked.

'I am. When I first mentioned the club cover to Archie, he didn't show any interest in investigating it. His line was that a couple of faint initials, if indeed that's what they were, hardly amounted to proof of murder. It wasn't until after he talked to Brodie that he decided something must be done.'

De Silva frowned. 'Why would Brodie deliberately spur Archie to action?'

'I don't know, but what do you say to finding out more about Brodie? Let me see what I can do. We have consular records at the Residence. I may be able to dig up any information he provided when he came to Ceylon. We also hold records of the men who served in south-east Asia during the Great War. Brodie may have been among them. He talks of having served in the army and certainly gives out the impression of having been around this part of the world man and boy. The records may not give us any clues, but it's worth a try.'

'What do you think about Brodie's alibi?'

'This business of preparing the accounts for the AGM with David Llewellyn that morning? I'm not sure. My impression of David Llewellyn is that he's always been rather in awe of Brodie. If Brodie asked Llewellyn to vouch for him, he might agree, especially if Brodie made up a plausible story.'

They were both still contemplating what that might be when Archie appeared from the clubhouse and they took their leave of each other.

CHAPTER 23

'So, Charlie Frobisher's offered to find out anything he can about Mark Brodie's background.'

De Silva had telephoned Jane from the police station to run through the morning's events for her. It had been locked when he returned, and there was no sign of Prasanna and Nadar.

'How much do you know about him already?'

'Not much, apart from the fact he's golf club secretary and works as an agent in the tea business. Frobisher doesn't think he's ever been married. At least, if he has, he keeps quiet about it. Apparently, he never mentions any family back in England or says much about his life there. Frobisher says that conversations with him usually revolve around golf and the business of the club.'

'How's Charlie Frobisher proposing to find out more?'

'I understand there are consular and military records at the Residence.'

'It will be very interesting to see what Charlie Frobisher comes up with.' She paused. 'If Jack didn't do it, have you considered the possibility there might be someone else in the family who stands to benefit from Bernard Harvey's death?'

'Elizabeth Harvey?'

'Yes. I doubt she'd do anything on her own – she's already assured of a comfortable life – but just suppose she's fallen for someone who's drawn her into a plan to kill her husband. Brodie perhaps? You said he was charming.'

It was true that quite apart from the business with the club cover, he was suspicious of Brodie's and Llewellyn's alibis. Of the two, Brodie was by far the most likely candidate for Elizabeth Harvey's affections. 'It's an interesting theory.'

'From Brodie's point of view, with Jack out of the way, she'd be a very wealthy woman.'

'I'll keep that one up my sleeve for now and concentrate on finding Jack.' De Silva sighed. 'I doubt it's going to be easy. It's a great pity Tom Duncan forced us into letting him go.'

'Never mind, dear. I'm sure he'll turn up.'

'I hope so. For the moment, the important thing is to tread carefully and not alarm him. If he's still in Nuala, I don't want him knowing we've investigated his locker before we've caught up with him.'

'Did you leave the clubs there?'

'Yes, in exactly the position we found them.'

'Then there's no reason why he should suspect anything. It's also unlikely that he'd want to be seen at the golf club before they've even buried his grandfather. That would definitely not look good. And if he does try to hide the evidence, you have plenty of witnesses to what you found, or rather didn't find, in the locker.'

'Anyway, I'd better go. Goodness knows where Prasanna and Nadar have got to. If they don't turn up soon, I'll go out and look for them. I need to get them onto searching for Jack. And I must telephone Singh at Hatton to ask him to keep an eye out too.'

'What about your lunch? Have you time to come home?'

'No, I'll get something later.'

As he rang off, he reflected it was equally possible that Jack had taken off for Kandy or even Colombo. He sighed.

He didn't relish the prospect of having to tell his old col-leagues or that idiot Jayaratne that his main suspect had given him the slip.

CHAPTER 24

De Silva got up from his desk and went to look out into the street. Still no sign of Prasanna or Nadar. He went back to his office and fell to considering Jane's idea. It was true that Bernard Harvey had been an unpopular man, and Elizabeth Harvey might well have been unhappy with him, but having differences with a husband was a long way from killing him. He cast his mind back to the evening when he and Frobisher had broken the news to her. Was it possible that her collapse had been staged to fool them? It was hard to penetrate her cool manner, although she had seemed genuinely distressed at having to wait to arrange the funeral. Again though, that might have been an act. Mark Brodie was a good-looking man and he had the charm that, by all accounts, Bernard Harvey lacked. But he was going to need more than a hunch if he was to take Jane's theory further.

Hearing sounds in the public room, he went out to investigate and found Nadar.

'Good afternoon, sir.'

De Silva glanced at the clock on the wall. Yes, it was afternoon and already, it seemed to have been an inordinately long day. His stomach reminded him that he had been too busy thinking about Jane's theory to eat any lunch.

'Where did you get to?' he asked irritably. 'And where's Sergeant Prasanna?'

'At the bazaar, sir. We both went there this morning to finish checking if all the stallholders have their licences.'

De Silva had forgotten that while there was nothing for them to do on the Harvey case, he'd put Prasanna and Nadar onto the job of verifying the licences the British required stallholders in the bazaar to pay for. It showed initiative that they were getting on with it without needing to be prompted.

'Any problems?' he asked, feeling a little contrite.

'Most were correct, sir, but a few packed up quickly and started to leave when they saw us coming.'

De Silva raised an eyebrow. 'Did you catch any of them?'

'Two, sir,' Nadar said proudly. 'We fined them a paisa each and told them it would be two next time, as you said.'

'Good work, Constable.'

Nadar beamed. 'Thank you, sir.'

'Why isn't Prasanna here with you?'

'He wanted to return to the bazaar to see if he can find any of the others, sir.'

'When he comes back, I have a more important job for the two of you. I want you to go around town and look for Jack Harvey. If you see him, don't approach him. Just come back here and tell me where he is.'

A puzzled frown creased Nadar's forehead. 'Why is that, sir?'

'There's new evidence against him, although he doesn't know it yet. And I don't want to frighten him off by acting too hastily.'

The frown gave way to another wide smile. 'I think I am able to help with that job already, sir.'

'What do you mean?'

'On my way back here, I saw a cream Rolls Royce with a lady driving it.'

De Silva knew of only one such car in Nuala. 'Was the lady good looking with dark hair cut in a short style?'

'Yes, sir.'

'Hmm, that must have been Elizabeth Harvey.'

'The car went by very quickly, sir, but a man who looked like Jack Harvey was with her.'

'What direction were they going in?'

'To the Crown Hotel. I saw the car drive up to reception. The lady and her passenger must have got out for it was one of the doormen who parked it.'

'And what time was this?'

'Just as I was coming back here, sir.'

De Silva clapped Nadar on the shoulder. 'You may have saved me a lot of time and trouble, Constable. Excellent work again. I'll be in my office. I have a call to make.'

One of the receptionists at the Residence answered his call. He waited a few minutes for Archie's gruff voice to come down the line.

'What news, de Silva?'

'My constable spotted the Harveys' Rolls Royce driving up to the Crown Hotel, sir. From his description, Elizabeth Harvey and Jack were in it. It wasn't long ago. They should still be there.'

'Sounds a reasonable deduction.' A sharp note entered Archie's voice. 'But I don't want a public scene. I'll get one of my staff here to telephone the hotel and make some excuse for wanting to know if the Harveys are there. If they are, I'll let you know. Best if you post yourself outside, somewhere discreet, and wait until they come out. After that, follow them home and make the arrest there. I'll send Frobisher to back you up.'

De Silva frowned. Much as he liked and admired Charlie Frobisher, what about his own men? After all, it was thanks to Nadar they had got this far.

'De Silva? Is something the matter?'

'With respect, sir, I'd prefer to take my constable with me.'

There was a pause; de Silva waited for a sharp retort. But none came. Archie's voice mellowed. 'Of course. And send him my compliments on his powers of observation.'

CHAPTER 25

An hour later, having received confirmation from the Residence that the Harveys hadn't left the hotel, de Silva parked the Morris in a far corner of the Crown's parking area, and he and Nadar settled down to wait. Half an hour passed before they saw Elizabeth Harvey emerge. She was alone. By the time her car had been brought up and she'd driven away, there was still no sign of Jack. De Silva wondered if the staff member at the Residence had been misinformed.

'We'll give it a few minutes,' he said to Nadar. 'He might have met a friend and decided to stay on for a while.'

The minutes ticked by. At last, Jack Harvey appeared with another man. They went over to a blue Packard and climbed in. Keeping at a discreet distance, de Silva followed them as they drove through town and took the road for the Harvey plantation. When the Packard reached the gates and was let through, de Silva pulled into a place beside the road where the Morris was partially hidden by trees.

'If Harvey's friend stays up at the plantation, we may have a long wait.' Hopefully, if Elizabeth Harvey hadn't already returned, she wouldn't turn up now before the fellow left. Arresting Jack with her present would be an unwelcome complication.

Fortunately, five minutes later, the Packard reappeared and set off back in the direction of town. De Silva waited until it was out of sight then eased the Morris up to the gates. The guard let them through. The Rolls Royce wasn't in the drive, but Jack's car was. They were halfway to the front door when he emerged from the house, car keys in hand.

He scowled. 'What are you doing here? Elizabeth's not at home, and I have to be somewhere in half an hour. There are funeral arrangements to make for my grandfather. At least you lot have had the decency to release his body at last.'

Instinctively, de Silva got between Jack and the red SSI Tourer. Jack's scowl intensified. 'Get away from my car. Haven't I said that I'm in a hurry?'

'Your appointment will have to wait, sir.'

'Having the nerve to tell me what to do is becoming a habit with you, Inspector, and a most inadvisable one. Now if you'll excuse me.' He tried to push past de Silva to get into his car, but de Silva held him back. Roughly, Jack shook him off and stared at him, eyes blazing. 'Get off my property,' he snapped.

Calmly, de Silva faced him. 'Certainly, but you're coming with us. You're under arrest.'

* * *

'The important thing is that Jack Harvey isn't going anywhere now. At least, not unless Tom Duncan gets him out on bail. But the application would have to be made to Archie in his capacity as local magistrate and I doubt he'd grant it.'

'Has Elizabeth Harvey been told?'

'If not, she soon will be. Archie undertook to do it.'

'What are you going to do now?'

'Eat another piece of this excellent walnut cake.'

Jane had recently shown their cook how to make the

English recipe, and de Silva had acquired a taste for it. It was rather late for tea, but it was the first time he'd had the chance to eat since breakfast at the golf club.

He let his gaze stray to the garden. Combined with the cool late afternoon breeze that had sprung up, the greenery soothed his weary eyes. A flock of blue magpies scuttled about in the trees, their rasping calls mingling with the squeaky-gate whistle of an unseen golden oriole It had been a long day. Thank goodness it had also been a productive one.

Jane cleared her throat. He looked across and saw her enquiring expression.

'Ah, yes. I'll have to question Jack again, although if he wants Tom Duncan present, it might be hard to get much out of him. There'll be statements to take from Archie, Brodie and Charlie Frobisher, and I must go down to Kandy too. Archie's still banging on about the importance of going myself to find out the truth about when Jack left the Blue Cat, and I know he's right. I need to speak to the manager. If he's lying as Jack claims he is, it puts a different complexion on matters, and I want to know who persuaded him to.'

Archie's stentorian tones still rang in his ears. No doubt he anticipated a lot of pressure from Duncan on behalf of his client.

'I don't want anything else going wrong though. To be on the safe side, I'll telephone someone other than Jayaratne and ask them to go around and find out for me when the manager's sure to be there.'

'Who will you ask?'

'I still have a few useful contacts in Colombo. I'm sure they can suggest someone in Kandy who'll oblige.'

Jane looked at him thoughtfully. 'Shanti, I know you've arrested him, but are you really sure Jack did it? I'm not convinced you are. What about Elizabeth Harvey and Mark Brodie? Has Charlie Frobisher managed to find anything out about him yet?'

'You know me too well,' he said with a smile. 'I do have my doubts. Brodie may just have wanted to help, but I'd still like to know more about him.'

The sound of the doorbell drifted from indoors.

'Were you expecting anyone?' asked de Silva.

'No.'

A moment later, one of the house servants appeared. 'Mr Frobisher is here, sahib. He would like to speak with you.'

De Silva frowned. He had expected Frobisher to telephone if he had any information. Coming in person looked serious.

'Ask him to come in.'

'Yes, sahib.'

'Do you want to see him on your own?' asked Jane.

'Of course not. And I'm sure you don't want me to either.'

'I must confess, I'm curious to find out what this is about.'

De Silva suddenly felt mildly guilty about being found relaxing on his verandah when Frobisher had probably been busy with investigations for the case. However, if Frobisher thought that he was slacking, he gave no indication of it.

'How nice to see you,' said Jane as the servant showed him in. 'Will you join us for a late tea?'

'Thank you, ma'am. Tea would be excellent.' He sat down, rubbing his hands. 'I understand you arrested Jack Harvey this afternoon. You found him very quickly.'

'A stroke of luck. Jane and I were just wondering how your investigations into Mark Brodie are going.'

'The boss kept me busy today, so I've had no time to look at any of our records, but there's been a development that might work in our favour. Mark Brodie has asked me if I'll partner him in a golf tournament down at Hatton the day after tomorrow. I've said I will.'

'Forgive me, but it's not clear to me how that will work in our favour.'

Frobisher put a large spoonful of sugar in his cup of tea and stirred it vigorously. 'The tournament goes on all day. It's a chance to search his bungalow.'

'What about the servants?'

'He has only one. I believe he was his batman in the war. Brodie doesn't seem to be the kind of man who likes home comforts. He eats most of his meals at the golf club. As far as I can tell, he only goes home to sleep.'

'That servant is likely to be there though. How do I avoid him?'

'I've thought of that. Brodie often speaks of him being a good mechanic. Learnt his trade in the war, apparently. I manoeuvred Brodie into offering me a lift to Hatton. Tomorrow night, I plan to go over to his bungalow. I'll wait until all the lights are off inside, then disable his car. It's easy to make it look as if something pretty important has simply rattled loose and got lost on a bumpy road. When I go over there in the morning, Brodie won't be able to start the car, so we'll have to take mine.'

De Silva was almost sorry for Brodie having to cope with a hair-raising journey to Hatton.

'As he'll have to look for replacements for the lost parts, the servant will be kept busy for an hour or so putting Brodie's car right. That will give you time to search the bungalow.'

'How clever of you!' Jane clapped her hands together.

Frobisher beamed. 'Thank you, Mrs de Silva.'

De Silva hadn't spoken. As a policeman, he ought not to condone criminal damage. Even if Brodie's man was able to repair the car quite easily, that was what it amounted to.

Jane and Charlie Frobisher were still discussing the idea. Eventually, she paused. 'You're very quiet, dear. Is something wrong?'

Should he quash the plan? Then again, it might produce some useful evidence, and it seemed watertight. The lack of any likelihood of being caught ought not to be the deciding factor, but for once, he would bend the rules.

'It's unorthodox to say the least, but we'll take a chance. If Mark Brodie's innocent, no one ever needs to know.'

'And if he's not,' said Frobisher, 'I'm sure we can smooth it over with the boss.'

'So, that's settled. Do you need my help with the car?'

'I think I can manage.'

'Is this kind of activity something they teach you at Civil Service college?'

Frobisher grinned. 'Some of the things we learn are rather unconventional, but I have to lay claim to this idea as my own. As a boy, I was very fond of reading spy stories. My father was an author and something of an eccentric. He often challenged my brothers and me to unravel the codes that he devised or get ourselves out of the tight spots he put us in. He liked to say it was for the purposes of research, but I think it may also have had something to do with our mother insisting he keep an eye on us when she was busy. My parents didn't employ many servants.'

If the family hadn't had much money, Frobisher had done well to get to Civil Service college. How had he managed it? Having a good brain wasn't always enough to get on.

'My uncle on my mother's side served in India for many years. He had contacts in the Colonial Service and helped me with my career.'

'Well, we're very glad he did, aren't we, Shanti?' said Jane.

'Indeed, we are.'

He looked down at Frobisher's plate, where all that was left of the large slice of walnut cake Jane had cut him was a few crumbs. Rather dismayed, he remembered the young man's gargantuan appetite at breakfast. He hoped Jane wouldn't press him to another slice. There might be none left.

CHAPTER 26

Elizabeth Harvey sat on her verandah, a coil of cigarette smoke rising into the evening air. The glorious sunset had faded, and the sky had taken on the pearl-grey sheen that would soon turn to black. A skein of geese flapped in the direction of the town lake. She watched the vivid green of the distant tea terraces start to merge with the darker shades of the jungle beyond.

What was she to do? She had it in her power to put an end to this business, but did she want to? She thought of the pampered life she'd lived and the new life that stretched before her. Would they be happy together? Or would she come to regret that she'd hidden the truth?

The geese were mere specks in the sky now; a solitary heron wheeled overhead, carried upwards by currents of air from the cooling earth.

More than anything, she dreaded being alone. There had always been someone to look after her, someone to provide the luxuries she craved. She had no regrets over Bernard's death; she had never loved him. But Jack? Feckless, charming, attractive Jack. He was so young.

She examined her nails. The varnish on one of them was chipped. For a moment, it distracted her, and she scowled. She hated not to look her best.

A small voice whispered in her ear. If she lost her looks, would *he* stay faithful?

Getting up, she went down the stone stairs that led onto the lawn and wandered over to the lily pond. Thick green pads of vegetation, studded with luscious pink and white flowers, covered most of the surface, leaving only small channels where Bernard's precious tropical fish cruised through the dark water, their iridescent scales gleaming as they darted after insects. She picked up a stone and tossed it in, scattering them to the far corners of the pond.

Slowly, the ripples subsided. The fish returned to feeding. Unlike them, if she spoke up, she could never turn back.

CHAPTER 27

De Silva parked the Morris as near as he dared to Mark Brodie's bungalow and got out to walk the last of the way. Frobisher's call late the previous evening had confirmed that the ground was prepared. Brodie's car was well and truly immobilised. Frobisher's breezy tones had evidenced the blithe confidence of the young. As he proceeded cautiously through the jungle however, there were butterflies in de Silva's stomach. What did people call it? The law of unintended consequences? He'd experienced too many occasions where the best laid plans had gone wrong.

He had unscrewed the Morris's wing mirrors before leaving her and also the windscreen wipers. At least he was able to take precautions against marauding monkeys. They were very fond of shiny things to play with. He'd learned to be cautious early in his days in the Hill Country where there was rarely a handy urchin about who would guard your car for you in return for a small fee. An early mistake had resulted in his coming back to the Morris to find six monkeys cavorting all over her, one of them brandishing a mirror and another ensconced in the driver's seat shredding a map that it had purloined from the glove compartment.

The trees thinned out as he reached the top of a low hill. Brodie's bungalow was not far away in the valley below. Dimly, he made out a red car coming along the road that led to it. It must be Charlie Frobisher's MG arriving to take him and Brodie off to their golf match.

Finding a handy log, he sat down to wait until he saw the MG leaving and mopped his face with his handkerchief. He wasn't as fit as he used to be, although the jungle was a severe test for anyone. Its humid air wrapped around you like a damp blanket, and it was all too easy to turn an ankle on the treacherous ground.

A colony of ants swarmed in the rough grooves of the log's bark. Ceylon was reputed to have hundreds of varieties of ants, and a lot of them were poisonous. Better to take no chances. He stood up and carried on to where the tree belt ended. From his vantage point, he would see the red MG setting off for Hatton.

There was no sign of Brodie's car. Maybe he kept it in the garage nearby. Once Brodie's servant had gone inside to fix it, he would circle around and approach the bungalow from the side, where he would be out of sight. He hoped Charlie Frobisher was right to be confident that the man would leave a door or window open. In case not, he'd brought his lock-picking kit.

The steady throb of insects, mingled with the songs of birds, provided the soundtrack to the wait. At last, the red MG started back down the bungalow's drive. There was no sign of Brodie's servant. Maybe he'd stayed in the garage with the car.

Cautiously, de Silva approached the bungalow. Sounds came from the garage. If the fellow was as good a mechanic as Frobisher said, he'd have to move fast.

At the back of the bungalow, all the windows were closed, and the only door locked, but it didn't take him long to deal with it. When it opened, a wave of trapped, hot air rolled out. He was in a small sunroom with a glass roof. The next room he came to was a little larger: a cross between a kitchen and scullery. It wasn't lavishly equipped, but everything was spotlessly clean and the pots and pans on the shelves were arranged with military precision. A refrigerator contained a small number of basic provisions, but then Charlie Frobisher had said that Brodie took most of his meals at the golf club.

Next came a sitting room that was neat but character-less, followed by a dining room that didn't look as if it had been used for years. Nothing in either of them was of any interest.

He peered through one of the remaining doorways and saw a bathroom. The next door led to a bedroom that must be Brodie's. The drawers were filled with neat piles of underwear, socks, handkerchiefs, and golf shirts. He checked through the drawers, trying to put everything back as he had found it. Hopefully, neither Brodie nor his servant would notice. After that, he turned his attention to the cupboard, which contained trousers, a few jackets, and pairs of everyday and golfing shoes. There was also a dinner suit that presumably Brodie needed for functions at the club and the Residence. He tried all the pockets but there was nothing in them. On the shelf at the top of the cupboard, there were a few hats.

The last room he came to was Brodie's study. Like his office at the golf club, it contained neatly arranged shelves of files and a large desk. His passport was in one of the desk drawers, along with a half-used bottle of ink, some sheets of blotting paper, paper clips, and a ball of rubber bands. Nothing one wouldn't expect to find.

De Silva sat down at the desk. This was going to be a waste of time. He would be sorry to disappoint Frobisher but perhaps it was for the best. Archie need never know about this breach of protocol.

He went to the window and opened it slightly, just able to glimpse the side of the garage. The sound of an engine starting came from inside. The servant must keep a range of tools and spares for Brodie's car. He must hurry. As he took a last glance around the room, a small shelf of books he hadn't noticed before caught his eye. He hadn't put Brodie down as a literary man and the titles confirmed it. There were several books on golf and a few adventure novels with lurid covers. Then one of the titles made him pause. It was a book of poetry. He pulled it out and flipped through the pages, wondering why Brodie had it in his collection. Turning to the flyleaf, he found a handwritten dedication: *To Mark, with all my love, E.*

"E" for Elizabeth Harvey perhaps? She didn't seem the kind of woman who read poetry, but love brought out unexpected traits in people. He looked again at the writing, remembering one of the teachers at the police college who had been keen on the study of handwriting. He claimed that the art of deducing a person's character traits from their handwriting had a very long pedigree. De Silva hadn't thought much of the idea at the time, but over his years in the force, it had sometimes provided a few clues. His teacher might have claimed this style of writing indicated someone who lacked confidence and struggled with life. It seemed an unlikely description of Elizabeth Harvey, but appearances were sometimes deceptive.

He slipped the book back in its place. As yet, he wasn't sure what to make of it, but it was an interesting find.

CHAPTER 28

'It's a good thing you went there,' said Jane when he told her what he'd found. 'Without this new angle on the case, Jack Harvey might have been wrongly convicted of his grandfather's murder.'

'We mustn't jump to conclusions, my love. The book is hardly conclusive proof that Mark Brodie and Elizabeth Harvey conspired to murder her husband. It might have been given to Brodie by someone else entirely. Anyway, the original idea was just speculation. We'll need more than that.'

Jane sighed. 'You're right, of course. But they would have a clear motive. She'd be immensely wealthy, and if she and Brodie married, so would he. As I've said before, killing his grandfather doesn't make much sense from Jack's point of view. He was already due to inherit, subject to the obligation to support Elizabeth during her lifetime. With what one's heard about Bernard Harvey's fortune, there's money for that with plenty left over.'

'True, but it's hard to know what goes on in people's heads. Jack may have resented his grandfather and wanted to escape from his shadow.'

'If he'd wanted that, why not leave the plantation and prove himself somewhere else?'

De Silva shrugged. 'I have no answer to that.'

'When are you going to Kandy? The case might appear

in a whole new light if Inspector Jayaratne's man's information turns out to be unreliable and you find out why.'

'Not yet, unfortunately. My contact came back to tell me the manager's away in Colombo. He'll keep an eye out and let me know when the fellow comes back.' He scratched his chin. 'I can do something that might help us though. I'll pay a visit to David Llewellyn instead. I'd like to see if I can shake his and Brodie's alibis. If Llewellyn admits he was covering for Brodie, it will be interesting to find out why and see what Llewellyn can tell me about his friend's activities.'

CHAPTER 29

An early morning telephone call to Llewellyn's office established that he was out at a meeting but would be returning in the afternoon. After that, de Silva paid a visit to his bungalow and spoke to his servants. He drove back to town in a thoughtful mood.

Llewellyn's office had a shabby frontage on a narrow street in one of the less salubrious parts of Nuala. A general air of decay hung about the place. De Silva remembered Charlie Frobisher mentioning there were rumours that Bernard Harvey had put some of Llewellyn's clients out of business.

The bell attached to the door jangled as he went in. A frowsy woman in a grey dress swiftly put the magazine she was reading into a drawer and asked if she could help him.

'I telephoned this morning about coming to speak to Mr Llewellyn.'

'Oh yes, Inspector de Silva. Wait here, please.'

She disappeared for a few moments and de Silva heard voices. It would be a nuisance if Llewellyn now claimed that he had no time to talk to him. He'd prefer not to have to force the issue and put the accountant on his guard.

'Mr Llewellyn will see you, but he doesn't have long.' De Silva doubted the receptionist's tone would have been as curt if he had been a Britisher.

Llewellyn's office was as chaotic as Mark Brodie's had

been tidy. Grimy windows let in a meagre amount of sunshine from the narrow street outside. A murky-looking cup of half-drunk tea stood on the desk among the jumble of paperwork and the air was stale with tobacco smoke. The office was a long way from the privileged comfort of the Royal Nuala Golf Club.

Llewellyn regarded him with a look of suspicion. 'How can I help you, Inspector?'

The receptionist obviously took her cue from her boss where civility was concerned. De Silva vowed that he wouldn't show his aggravation. He sat down in the chair opposite Llewellyn.

'My apologies for taking up your time. The matter I would like to discuss is, however, a serious one.'

Llewellyn laced his fingers. 'Go on.'

'You told me at our last meeting that you and Mr Brodie were at your home doing some work on the accounts for a forthcoming meeting the morning that Bernard Harvey's murder took place.'

'That's correct. I understand his grandson, Jack, has been arrested. A shocking affair. Poor old Harvey was very good to him.'

'Are you absolutely sure you and Mr Brodie met at your home, not here in the office?'

'I've told you. We met at my home.'

'For the purposes of the trial, I'll need a formal statement to that effect.'

'So, you've come to take it now, I assume. I would have appreciated more notice, but we'd better get on with it.'

'In due course.'

'What do you mean?' A wary look came into Llewellyn's eyes.

'I'm sure I don't need to remind you, Mr Llewellyn, just how important it is to be absolutely truthful in these matters. You'll be required to swear to the truth of your statement in court. Anything less than a scrupulous account of the facts would expose you to the full rigours of the law.'

The accountant shuffled in his seat. Beads of sweat glistened on his forehead. Compared with his fellow committee members, Tom Duncan and Brodie himself, it was clearly not all that hard to get under the man's skin.

'Are you absolutely sure there's nothing in your story that you'd like to change?'

Llewellyn lumbered to his feet. 'Of course not. Now if you'll excuse me, I have a client arriving any minute.'

De Silva raised a hand. 'Just one more moment, sir.'

'What for?' snapped Llewellyn.

'I'd be obliged if you would explain to me why your servants say you left for the office as usual that morning and didn't return until the evening.' He had been obliged to exert considerable pressure before they reluctantly revealed their employer's activities. Servants were always anxious for their jobs.

Llewellyn purpled. 'You had no business questioning them. Their memories are very likely unreliable in any case.'

'In the space of a few days? I hardly think so, sir.'

The stuffing went out of Llewellyn; his face took on a grey tinge. 'I tell you, they're wrong.'

'They had no reason to lie, sir.' He paused. 'Wouldn't it be easier to tell me the truth?'

A range of emotions flitted over Llewellyn's face. 'Very well,' he said at last. 'Brodie won't like it, but that can't be helped. He's been having an affair.'

De Silva's ears pricked up. 'Who's the lady?'

'Tom Duncan's wife, Ella. I can't say I blame her. Brodie says that bastard Duncan treats her badly. Even knocks her about sometimes.'

An image of Tom Duncan's thin lips, cold eyes and brutal manner rose in de Silva's mind.

'She's neurotic, of course. Brodie's no saint – Ella's far

from being the first woman in his life – but he tried to help her. In the end though, it got too much for him and he decided to break the whole thing off. He tried to let her down gently, but she reacted badly. Her behaviour became a major concern. As ill luck would have it, it was on the morning that Harvey was killed that he'd gone to see her to try and talk her out of doing anything foolish. When the Harvey business blew up, he asked me to cover for him. If anyone found out he and Ella had been seeing each other, it would make trouble for them both, especially Ella.'

From what he'd seen of Brodie, de Silva wondered if Llewellyn credited his friend with more kindness than he possessed. It was very convenient too that the visit had taken place on the day Bernard Harvey was murdered. Other things were suspicious as well. Tom Duncan said he left home that morning around midday and Ella confirmed it. Had she gone to meet Brodie, simply assuming when she returned that her husband was going out for the first time that morning? But where would she meet Brodie and how would she have got there? And why choose a morning when Duncan would be at home and likely to ask where she was going? It seemed more probable that Brodie was lying to Llewellyn about his movements, but he wasn't about to reveal that to the accountant at the moment.

Hunched in his chair, Llewellyn had sunk into morose silence. 'Does Brodie have to know I've told you?' he asked at last.

'Not yet, and maybe never. For now, I strongly advise you to say nothing about it to anyone. Failure to abide by that may result in your being prosecuted for interfering in the course of justice.'

De Silva wasn't absolutely sure Clutterbuck would support that, but he hoped it sounded daunting enough to keep Llewellyn quiet.

'I'll say nothing.' Llewellyn gave de Silva a pleading

look. 'The golf club's everything to me. I don't want a black mark against my name.'

CHAPTER 30

'How sad,' said Jane when he returned to Sunnybank to tell her what he'd learnt from Llewellyn. She frowned. 'Why didn't I think of it when we talked about the book of poetry you found in Brodie's study? I'd put money on Ella Duncan having given it to him. I remember Florence telling me that she loves poetry. Poor lady, she must be feeling wretched. It's no wonder she was behaving so strangely when Emerald and I went to visit her that time.'

'Did you tell me about that?'

'With so much going on, I forgot, and at the time, it didn't seem relevant to the case. Both Emerald and I were convinced she was deeply troubled about something. It's never been easy to talk to her, but that day it was even more difficult than usual. It must have been around the time when she found out Mark Brodie wanted to break with her. I'm sure she'll be better off without him in the long run though. He doesn't sound to be the kind of man she needs, and even if he was, divorcing her husband wouldn't be easy.'

'The question is, did Brodie end the affair purely because of Ella Duncan's behaviour, or was he already transferring his attentions to Elizabeth and planning to kill Harvey?'

'How are we to find that out?'

'I don't know yet, but you've reminded me, I need to check the rest of Elizabeth's alibi. We know she lunched at the Crown that day, but I've yet to visit the clinic in Hatton where she said she spent the morning.'

He looked at his watch. 'There's time for that today.'

* * *

The Victoria Clinic was discreetly tucked away in a quiet street in Hatton. Unlike David Llewellyn's office, it breathed money and privilege. De Silva suspected that it made a great deal more money than the good Doctor Hebden's practice.

An immaculately coiffured receptionist in a smart uniform greeted him frostily when he walked in. It was no surprise that she declined to give him any information without one of the doctors authorising it. 'And all of them are engaged with patients this afternoon,' she said. 'I'm afraid you may have a long wait.'

He assured her it wasn't a problem.

The waiting room he was shown to was furnished with comfortable armchairs upholstered in chintz. A neat stack of British magazines was arranged on a low table; tasteful paintings decorated the pristine walls. The air had a floral scent with a mildly antiseptic undertone. To pass the time, he flipped through one of the magazines.

After half an hour, he decided that either the clinic had a great many patients, or they needed extremely long appointments or both. His eyelids drooped and the magazine slipped from his lap to the floor. No, he mustn't doze off.

In a corner of the room, a small electric fan made an inadequate attempt to cool the air. He got up and tried to open the window, but it was locked. There must be a gap somewhere though. A small blue butterfly had found its way in and was fluttering against the glass. Eventually, it sank exhausted to the windowsill and lay twitching feebly. If this waiting went on much longer, he'd be in a similar state.

At last, he heard footsteps and the receptionist returned. 'No one is available to see you this afternoon. I'm sorry you had to wait.'

De Silva suppressed his irritation. 'Then I'd like to make an appointment for the morning.'

'All of the doctors are busy tomorrow.' The receptionist's expression was impassive.

This was obviously going to be a game he was unlikely to win without making more fuss than he wanted to. On his way out, he glanced at the reception counter. The appointment book was tantalisingly close, and it probably contained all the information he needed. The only problem was, how to have it to himself for a few moments.

In the street, he found the window for the reception area and waited, careful to stand out of sight. If the receptionist left her desk, he might just have time to slip back in and check the book.

Minutes passed. He had almost given up the idea when she stood up from her desk and left the room. He'd have to move quickly. Inside, he hurried to the counter and pulled the book towards him. Thumbing through the pages, he had just reached the one he wanted when he heard the click of the receptionist's heels. He ran his eye down the page. Elizabeth Harvey was booked in for a morning appointment. Closing the book, he took a few speedy steps back to the door.

The receptionist looked surprised; then suspicious. He pulled his notebook out of his pocket. 'Forgive me if I alarmed you. I left this in your waiting room.'

She frowned. 'I'm sure I didn't notice it when I went past just now.'

'Ah, it's a very small book. Easy to miss.'

He smiled as he sidled backwards out of the door. 'Good day to you, ma'am.'

CHAPTER 31

'I'll ask Emerald what goes on at the Victoria Clinic,' said Jane. 'I expect she'll be able to tell me. She's turning into quite the doctor's wife already. In my experience, they always know everything.'

'Mm.'

De Silva had already lost interest in the Victoria Clinic. His mind was on his trip to Kandy the following day. The fact that Elizabeth Harvey's alibi had stood up exonerated her from a direct role in her husband's murder. Nonetheless, she and Brodie might have planned it together. If, however, they were innocent, and Jack had lied about the time he left the Blue Cat, the finger still pointed at him.

* * *

The following morning, having heard from his contact that the manager of the Blue Cat had returned, de Silva took the train to Kandy and settled down to enjoy the view as rolling tea terraces gave way to lowlands vivid with paddy fields. The train was delayed, so it was evening when it steamed into Kandy station. The Blue Cat would probably be busy; best to catch the owner in the morning when he might be off-guard after a long night's work.

He found a place to stay and used their telephone to call Jane to tell her he had arrived late and would have to stay overnight. Afterwards, he ventured out to have dinner, but first, he took a stroll beside the town's lake, the beautiful expanse of water known as The Sea of Milk. People said the surrounding white parapet resembled a ring of clouds. Hoarse croaking sounds drew his attention to the stocky night herons waiting by the water, each with their own patch of territory. They were adept night hunters, feeding on the shellfish, lizards and frogs that inhabited the lake.

The image of David Llewelyn rose in his mind. If he hadn't helped to lay a false trail, the case might have been closer to being solved by now, with Mark Brodie emerging as a suspect. Would he have to answer for his lie, even if it hadn't been uttered with criminal intent? Archie would probably take his time considering what to do. Eventually the matter might be forgotten.

He needed food to take away the sour taste the thought left in his mouth. Leaving the lake, he walked to a small cafe he knew. They served simple but tasty food, and he chose a selection of curried vegetables with rice, accompanied by a large round of well-charred naan bread, glistening with clarified butter. Later, after another stroll to clear his head, he returned to the hotel and bed.

The unfamiliar noises of the city and thoughts of the next day's visit kept him awake for a while. It was two o'clock in the morning before his eyes closed, and he over-slept. Dressing hurriedly, he snatched a quick breakfast in the hotel dining room, left the overnight bag he had taken the precaution of bringing with him with the receptionist and headed for the Blue Cat.

A sleepy doorman looked at his badge and let him in. Inside, two young women wearing loose cotton robes unfastened over their night clothes sat at the bar smoking and drinking tea. From their tousled hair and the shadows around their eyes, they looked as if they'd had a late night. Taking one look at de Silva's uniform, they slid off their barstools and vanished through a door at the back.

Rapping on the counter, de Silva called out. 'Service!'

While he waited, he surveyed the room. Peeling paint made leprous patches on its black walls. The lights strung across them might have given the place an air of glamour at night, but in the harsh light of day, they looked tawdry. The wiring was worryingly frayed in places too.

There had been many places like it in Colombo. Part of his job had been to keep an eye on some of them, to ensure they weren't death traps and abided more or less by the rules the British laid down for gambling and selling alcohol. It had been a tedious task. A club would be closed down for breaching the regulations, only to open up somewhere else a few months later under a new name. Most of them hadn't really been doing much harm, provided the alcohol they peddled wasn't adulterated with anything that rotted the gut.

He noticed some papers on the bar. Amongst them were bills addressed to Mr V S Patel at the Blue Cat. He studied the array of bottles on the shelves behind: Scotch whisky, Gordon's gin, vermouth, Cinzano, and numerous sticky bottles that looked like liqueurs. There were also bottles of local beers and British imports. They looked genuine enough.

A short, rotund man dressed in crumpled shirt and trousers appeared, scratching himself under one arm. He was unshaven and looked as if, like the two women who had so hastily left, he too had been up most of the night. He squinted at de Silva. 'What can I do for you, Inspector?'

'Are you the owner, Mr Patel?'

'Yes.'

'Then I hope you can help me. I'm making enquiries about one of your regulars. His name is Jack Harvey.'

'One of your officers was asking questions about Mr Harvey a few days ago. I told him everything I knew then. There's nothing to add.'

'I didn't send the officer, so I'd like you to tell me again.'

A belligerent look came over the owner's face. He folded his arms. De Silva was sure there was something familiar about him. He searched his memory: V S Patel – the name definitely rang a bell.

'I can come back with a warrant, or we can deal with this now,' he said calmly. Detecting a shifty look in the owner's eyes, it came to him who he was. He had run one of the clubs in Colombo that had been shut down for hosting illegal gambling and other activities. 'We've met before,' he said. 'You haven't always been in Kandy, have you? You had a club in Colombo.'

'You're thinking of my cousin,' the owner said quickly. 'Many people say we are as alike as two grains of rice. Even my wife. He's the one who had the club in Colombo, but he's not there any longer. He went away to the north.'

'Two grains of rice, eh?' De Silva smiled. He surveyed the room, giving the owner time to sweat a little. 'You have an interesting place here,' he said at last. 'Larger than the club I remember in Colombo. You must be doing well. I'd like to take a look around.'

'There's nothing out of order.' A note of panic came into the owner's voice.

'Then you'll have no problem showing me.' De Silva paused. 'Unless you'd prefer to answer my questions first.'

Reluctantly, the owner nodded.

'Does Jack Harvey often come here?'

'Now and then.'

'How often is now and then? Once a week? Once a month?'

'More like every week,' muttered the owner.

'Was he in the Thursday before last?'

'Yes, I told the other officer that.'

'Was his behaviour any different from usual?'

The owner looked puzzled. 'In what way different?'

'Was he quieter than usual? Drinking more? Did he spend the time alone or with other people?'

'He talks to a few people. That Thursday evening was no different. Whisky is his drink – four or five doubles maybe.'

It was more than de Silva would drink, but he knew many of the British in Ceylon were heavy drinkers. 'Does he spend time with any of your girls?'

'Sometimes. They entertain many of my customers. Only talking of course.'

'Of course.'

'I don't allow any funny business.'

'What time did he leave on Thursday?'

'About eleven o'clock.'

'You're certain?'

The owner's chin jutted. 'Yes.'

'I see. I'm glad we appear to have that cleared up. Now, I'd like to look around before I go. Shall we start upstairs?' He took a step in the direction of the wooden staircase in a dark corner of the bar.

'Maybe—' The owner tensed. 'Maybe, I am mistaken.'

'You were thinking of a different evening, perhaps?'

'Yes. He may have stayed later that Thursday.'

'How late?'

'I'm not sure.'

'Until Friday morning?'

'He might have,' the owner said reluctantly.

De Silva smiled. 'That wasn't so hard, was it?'

The unhappy expression didn't leave the owner's face.

'Who told you to say Jack Harvey left earlier?'

'There was a telephone call.'

'Who from?'

'It's hard to remember.'

With a sigh, de Silva rolled his eyes. 'My patience is wearing thin, but I'll ask you one more time. Who was it from?'

'One of the backers of the club.'

'Is his name Mark Brodie?'

'Yes.' With a shrug, the owner splayed his hands. 'He said it was a small favour to a friend. Nothing of any importance. The officer who came didn't ask many questions. He was in a hurry to leave.'

Who had Jayaratne sent? Some unfortunate rookie, no doubt, who had been easily fobbed off. De Silva frowned. 'It was not a small thing, but you don't need to know about that. All you need to know is that it's of the utmost importance that this conversation goes no further. Do I make myself clear?'

'Yes.'

'Good.'

A hopeful light came into the owner's eyes. 'Do you need to see everything now?'

De Silva shook his head. 'It will keep until another time.'

CHAPTER 32

Impatient as he was to be back in Nuala, de Silva had to wait for the night train. He debated going to the police station in Kandy, finally deciding not to. It was always possible that the club owner was up to no good, but Kandy was Jayaratne's patch. Up to that old donkey to keep it tidy. Doubtless, Jayaratne wouldn't appreciate interference anyway, and de Silva had more pressing matters to deal with.

Next morning, at Nanu Oya, where the line ended, he collected the Morris and drove on to Nuala. He would go first to the police station. He wanted Prasanna and Nadar with him as backup. It was clear to him now that Mark Brodie had tried to frame Jack Harvey for his grandfather's murder. That being the case, it was a reasonable deduction that Brodie had killed Harvey himself. And when it came to an arrest, he was the kind of man who was likely to put up a fight. He ought to tell Archie what had happened. He would telephone him from the police station.

Prasanna and Nadar were there when he arrived. 'Mrs Harvey has just telephoned, sir,' said Prasanna. 'She asked if you would come up and see her as soon as you returned.'

Elizabeth Harvey calling? An interesting development. Perhaps it was about Jack. On the other hand, if she was involved with Brodie, it might be a trap. He made a spur of the moment decision not to speak to Archie just yet. This was going to be his own show. Jack would have to languish under house arrest at the Residence for a little longer.

'Right, we'll get up there straight away. You two had better come with me. And be ready for anything. I'll explain on the way.'

He put his foot down and they reached the Harveys' plantation in record time. The Rolls Royce was the only car in the drive. Leaving Nadar outside to raise the alarm if Brodie turned up, de Silva parked the Morris as much out of sight as possible, then he and Prasanna went in.

'I'll do the talking. You keep your eyes open,' de Silva muttered. 'We may have trouble on our hands.'

Elizabeth Harvey waited for them in the drawing room. Her face was less carefully made up than when de Silva had last seen her, and her hair lacked its former glossy sheen.

'I understand you want to talk to me, ma'am.'

'Yes. I telephoned the Residence, but Archie Clutterbuck wasn't there.' A spasm of pain crossed her face. 'I should have said something straight away when he told me about the arrest; something I should have said long before now. You may have already guessed, Inspector, that it concerns my stepson, Jack.'

Intently, de Silva waited to hear what she would say next.

'He had nothing to do with Bernard's murder. Mark Brodie led everyone to believe it because it suited us. But I can't let Jack suffer for something he didn't do. Despite his faults, he loved his grandfather and Bernard cared deeply for him. If he was to be convicted—'

Her voice died away. They all knew that a conviction carried the death sentence.

A surge of relief went through de Silva. Instinct had served him well. He was on the right track at last. Brodie and Elizabeth Harvey were in this together. It surprised him that although she was clearly distressed, she didn't seem afraid. If she and Brodie had conspired to murder her husband, one or both of them would suffer the same fate as Jack Harvey would have done.

She shook her head. 'I know what you're thinking, Inspector. You're wrong. Mark and I have been lovers for some time, but neither of us killed my husband. We have no idea who did. Implicating Jack was simply convenient. On the morning Bernard was killed, Mark and I were together at his bungalow. We often met there when Bernard went to the golf club on Friday mornings.'

'You mean with Jack out of the way, the two of you would inherit the plantation and your late husband's fortune?'

'That was Mark's plan,' she said quietly. 'I wasn't happy with it, but it happened so quickly after Bernard was killed. There was no time to think straight. When Mark decides something—'

De Silva could believe Mark Brodie was a hard man to resist, yet a man's life had been at stake.

'I was afraid of what he'd do if I tried to stop him,' she ended wretchedly. She gave de Silva an imploring look. 'Inspector, I've told you the truth. Mark and I are innocent of Bernard's murder.'

Whether that was true or not, by her own admission, they were guilty of conspiring to pervert the course of justice, thought de Silva. Still, he had to admire her. It had taken courage to admit what she and Brodie had done. Her resolve to save Jack despite everything showed a side to her character that he hadn't expected. Was it the case that, in her heart, she hadn't fully trusted Brodie? How much did she know about Ella Duncan? David Llewellyn had mentioned there had been many others before her too. Perhaps Elizabeth feared a time would come when Brodie would leave her, or only stay for her money. Or worse still, find some way of appropriating it for himself.

He heard footsteps. Nadar appeared in the doorway, a bewildered servant hot on his heels.

'There's a black Jaguar coming up the drive, sir.'

It must be Brodie.

Elizabeth Harvey's hand went to her mouth. 'He'll see your car.'

'Perhaps. I suggest you leave us to meet him on our own, ma'am.'

After a moment's hesitation, she nodded. 'I'll go into the garden.'

De Silva braced himself. 'Stay out of sight behind that door, Nadar. And you, Prasanna, get yourself behind that sofa over there. If things get nasty, you may need to surprise him.'

'Elizabeth!' Brodie's voice came from the hall. He walked into the room and stopped abruptly. 'What are you doing here, Inspector?'

'I might ask you the same question, sir.'

His urbanity resurfacing, Brodie relaxed. 'I'm here as a concerned friend. Bernard Harvey and I knew each other well. He would have wanted me to rally round. There's a lot to attend to. Not least, the funeral.'

De Silva had to admire his quick thinking.

'Are you here to ask Elizabeth more questions?' Brodie went on. 'With respect, don't you think she's been through enough? Isn't it time she was left in peace to grieve?'

'It's fortunate you've come, sir. Mrs Harvey has given me some interesting information. However, I would like to hear your side of the story.'

'My side?' Brodie frowned. 'I can't imagine what you're talking about.' He strode to the door of the verandah. 'Elizabeth? Are you out there?'

De Silva followed him. The smell of her perfume betrayed that Elizabeth Harvey was close by. He sensed she was holding her breath.

Turning, Mark Brodie scowled. 'What have you done with her? I demand to know.'

'Mr Brodie, I've been down to Kandy. The owner of the Blue Cat club told me that you instructed him to lie about the time Jack Harvey left the club. I believe you gave a false alibi and also planted incriminating evidence, the club cover to be precise, out on the golf course, in an attempt to implicate Jack in his grandfather's murder.'

'This is outrageous!' spat Brodie. 'How dare you suggest I've fabricated evidence. It's plain as day that Jack Harvey's guilty.'

'No, Mark.'

Elizabeth Harvey stepped into the room. 'It's no use. The inspector knows we tried to put the blame for Bernard's murder on Jack.'

For a moment, fury contorted Brodie's face, then he recovered. 'Elizabeth, you don't know what you're saying. Grief has a way of confusing people. Jack killed his grandfather. I understand how much distress it causes you, but he must answer for his crime.'

He turned to de Silva, 'Inspector, I assure you, I've never spoken to anyone at this club in Kandy. Nor did I plant that cover on the course.'

'You had the opportunity. And the owner of the Blue Cat was very sure of what you told him to do. Do you also deny you are one of the club's financial backers? It's difficult never to have spoken to anyone there if you are.'

'So you'd refuse to take the word of a gentleman over the owner of some grubby club, and the ramblings of a woman whose mind is confused by grief, would you?'

'I'm not confused, Mark. I just can't let Jack take the blame for a crime he didn't commit.'

Brodie's eyes narrowed. He seized Elizabeth Harvey's wrist. 'Shut up, you silly bitch.'

She snatched her hand back and slapped him. For a moment, he clutched his cheek, then lunged at her. As if from nowhere, Prasanna leapt to help de Silva overpower him. Her face ashen, Elizabeth Harvey backed away.

'Mark Brodie,' said de Silva panting, 'I'm arresting you on a charge of murder. And I'm arresting you both on a charge of attempting to pervert the course of justice.'

CHAPTER 33

'How did Archie take it?' asked Jane.

She and de Silva were strolling by the town lake. They had driven down there in the cool of the late afternoon. His day had been spent writing up reports on recent events, then up at the Residence, explaining everything to Archie.

'Better than I expected.'

He picked up a stone and shied it at the water; it skipped across in a series of hops before sinking. Archie's reaction had been a relief. He was all too aware that his boss wasn't always as relaxed about being kept out of the loop with crimes that involved the British.

'I think the departure of the ambassador's party has been a relief,' he said with a grin. 'The prospect of an end to the formality it entailed seems to have put him in a good mood.'

Jane smiled. 'From what I hear, he's had to put up with a considerable amount of it while they were here. Hopefully, he won't cause problems now that he's free to involve himself in the case again.'

'It might not be a bad thing if he has any good ideas,' said de Silva with a sigh. 'If Brodie and Elizabeth Harvey are telling the truth, we may still have a long way to go.'

'What will happen to them?'

'Archie will decide that in his capacity as magistrate. If the charge of murder is ruled out, there'll still be the charge of attempting to pervert the course of justice.'

A fruit vendor was pedalling along the shore, stopping to offer mangos and pineapples to people taking a late stroll like the de Silvas. He smelt the delicious fruity smell on the warm air and fished a coin out of his pocket. 'Shall we have some?'

'I'm sure we have plenty of fruit at home.'

'But those mangos look particularly good.'

'Then buy a few if you want.'

He came back shaking his head. 'Overripe. I bought a pineapple instead.'

Putting it to his nose, he sniffed. Sweet and tart at the same time. And with its hairy, angular outside, needing care when you prepared it for eating. Then after all the effort, there was very little left compared with what you had started with. Much like this case, he thought glumly. There was something he was missing. If only he could work out what it was.

They returned home, and as he drifted off to sleep later that night, it crossed his mind that it might be worth finding a way of questioning Ella Duncan without her husband being present. If she and Brodie had met in secret that morning, it would prove his innocence.

CHAPTER 34

The following morning, Jane was in the kitchen discussing dinner with the cook when there was a telephone call. She was pleased to find that it was Ella Duncan. Perhaps she was prepared to accept some friendly help after all.

'Good morning, Mrs Duncan; how nice to hear from you. What can I do for you?'

There was a long pause.

'Mrs Duncan? Are you still there? Is something the matter?'

Ella Duncan spoke in a low voice. 'Mrs de Silva, I'm sorry to call you like this, but I didn't know who else to turn to. I need your help.'

'Of course, I'll do whatever I can.'

Another silence ensued. 'Mrs Duncan? Where are you? Would you like me to come and find you?'

'No!' Ella Duncan sounded agitated. 'You mustn't, but I want you to tell your husband that I know who killed Bernard Harvey.'

Jane frowned. Was this going to be a denunciation of Mark Brodie? If so, it had to be suspect. She waited for Ella to continue.

'It was my husband.'

* * *

'She ended the call very suddenly and I didn't want to tele-phone her back in case she had a good reason for that. I thought the best thing to do was to call you.'

'You did the right thing,' said de Silva. 'It's uncanny, but just before you rang, I realised what I've been missing all along. Ella Duncan wasn't telling the truth about the time her husband left home, but it had nothing to do with Mark Brodie. She was lying to cover up for Duncan. Did she explain why he killed Harvey?'

'Yes. She told me that he wanted to punish Mark Brodie by having him blamed for the crime.'

'Brodie? What does Brodie have to do with Duncan?'

'It's a long story, and it wasn't always easy to understand what Ella Duncan was saying. I think she was afraid of being overheard, but as far as I could gather, Duncan was brought up in India by family friends after his parents died in a car crash. His adopted family had two daughters. One of them called Virginia, and the other Jenny, whom he adored. When Duncan was eighteen, he went to England to study law, but when the war broke out, he joined up and was sent to fight in France. After the war, he returned to India. His adopted parents told him that Jenny had fallen ill and died. It was a long time before he learnt the truth was that she'd been expecting a baby. When her parents found out, they wanted her to get rid of it. She thought the father would marry her and refused. The father was Mark Brodie, whom she met after Duncan had left.'

'And did they marry?'

'No. By then Brodie was in the army like Duncan. When the war ended, it was too late. Jenny had died in childbirth and the baby too. Duncan blamed Brodie for everything.'

'Did you believe her story?'

'She sounded as if she was telling the truth. She admitted that she'd been having an affair with Brodie, and Duncan found out. Their marriage has been unhappy for a long time. She was sure he'd been watching Elizabeth and Brodie since their relationship began and knew when they usually met. She had no idea, though, that Duncan planned to kill Elizabeth's husband to incriminate Brodie. When they moved up to Nuala a couple of years ago, he said it was because it was better for his business to be near to where Bernard Harvey lived as Harvey was such an important client; now she thinks that wasn't the real reason. He must have found out that Brodie was here and hoped to find a way of punishing him.' Jane paused.

'Duncan made her lie about when he left home on the day Harvey was killed, but she didn't think much of it at the time. He said something about a business meeting that it was important he keep private. Later, all she could think about was that with Bernard Harvey dead, there was nothing to stop Mark and Elizabeth being together. It wasn't until Duncan told her that Jack had been set free and Mark arrested in his place, that she had a feeling there was something going on. There was such a note of triumph in Duncan's voice, and he never showed emotion over his work. She started to think that he'd been behaving oddly – for one thing, he didn't usually make such a fuss about having backache. It occurred to her that he wanted people to think he'd been in no state to attack anyone. She already knew part of the story, and she got the rest out of him. He swore that if she tried to tell anyone, he'd say she was delusional and have her locked up. She believed him; she knows he has medical evidence that she's suffered from mental problems and depression, and he'd cite her affair with Brodie.'

'But for Duncan to kill two innocent men—' de Silva's forehead creased.

'Yes, she was shocked when she heard the caddy was dead, but she claimed Duncan's conscience would be unlikely to trouble him over that. As for Bernard Harvey, what mattered to Duncan above everything was the chance to destroy Brodie. Even though Brodie had left her, she couldn't bear to think of his life being in danger. Despite the risk to herself, she decided to telephone me in secret.'

'But why would Duncan wait all this time?'

'Apparently, while Jenny's parents were alive, they insisted what had happened was kept a secret, but they're both dead now. Duncan claimed that his sister, Virginia, told him the story very recently. Ella said that if she'd been thinking straight, she would have guessed that wasn't true. Virginia and her family live in England and Duncan has almost no contact with them. Ella believes the sister told him when he went back to England for his mother's funeral and he's been wanting revenge ever since.'

De Silva remembered the photographs in the Duncans' bungalow. The pretty girl must have been Jenny, the other one the sister, Virginia. Had she been jealous of her sister and revealed the story to Tom Duncan out of spite? Duncan had played his hand cleverly. The murder had been laid at Mark Brodie's door as he'd hoped.

'Do you know where Ella is now?'

'I think she was at home, so she may still be there. Shanti, she seems really afraid of her husband. Whatever shall we do?'

'I don't want to risk barging in there. It might do more harm than good. This time, I must talk to Archie first.'

* * *

'You're lucky, you've caught him,' said Charlie Frobisher. 'He was planning to take the afternoon off and go up to the golf club. As the American ambassador and his party have just left, and Elizabeth Harvey and Mark Brodie are being held down at Kandy, he's keen to make up for lost time.

Between ourselves, I think he also wants to clear his head before tackling the case. I expect you'll be glad of some time to prepare too. By the way, one thing puzzles me. How did Elizabeth Harvey manage to be in two places at once? In the reports you wrote for Archie, you said her alibi for the Friday morning was good, but if she was at the Victoria Clinic, how could she be with Brodie too?'

De Silva squirmed. At least it was Charlie, not Archie, asking the question. He wished now that he hadn't mentioned the Victoria Clinic in his report. He strongly suspected he might have been too hasty, and the truth was that Elizabeth Harvey had been with Brodie.

'I'm afraid that may be a mistake on my part. I noticed Mrs Harvey's name in the appointment book at the clinic and assumed she had attended.'

'So, are you saying no one at the clinic actually confirmed that she did?'

'Well, they didn't in so many words.'

'Easy enough to check, I imagine.'

He chuckled when de Silva explained his difficulty. 'Leave it with me. Was it the case that you were ringing about, or is there something else?'

When de Silva ended his explanation, Frobisher let out a low whistle. 'Well, I'll be damned. You'd better get up here right away.'

* * *

A somnolent air hung over the Residence's grounds as he drove up to the front door. Gardeners hoed the flowerbeds in a desultory manner. Two of the cats the Clutterbucks kept to control vermin basked on top of a wall. Bees buzzed in the lavender beneath.

Charlie Frobisher met him on the steps. In the

mid-afternoon heat, even he seemed to have less energy than usual.

'The boss is in his study. I'm to come with you. I hope you have no objection.'

'None at all.'

'It seems quiet now the Americans have gone,' observed Charlie as they walked down the corridor and stopped at the study door. Archie Clutterbuck called out for them to come in. He looked weary, and de Silva felt quite sorry for him.

'Sit down, sit down. I hear there's been an unexpected development. You'd better tell me all about it, de Silva.'

Settling himself in one of the chairs opposite Archie, he felt a damp nose touch the back of his hand. He leant down and scratched Darcy behind the ears. The old Labrador grunted appreciatively before returning to his place by his master.

Archie listened carefully to what de Silva had already told Charlie Frobisher. 'Seems rather drastic, and not very good for business, to murder his own client in the process,' he said when de Silva had finished.

'Indeed, sir.'

'I believe the relationship was often difficult, sir,' interposed Frobisher. 'Duncan may not have been reluctant to lose Bernard Harvey as a client. He was probably confident Jack would keep him on and be far more malleable.'

'Hmm, I see. Go on.'

'It might have been a gamble on Duncan's part that Brodie and Mrs Harvey would be at Brodie's place together on the morning that he, Duncan, killed Bernard Harvey. He knew Brodie would be up at the club to welcome the American party, but he wouldn't be staying to play golf. Ella Duncan wasn't sure if her husband had taken the precaution of checking that Brodie and Mrs Harvey were engaged in their usual tryst, but my guess is that a man like Duncan wouldn't have overlooked the precaution. According to his wife, he'd been watching them for some time. That being the case, he would have known that Brodie would need to manufacture an alibi or come clean. The latter was very unlikely.'

'So, Brodie fell for the trick, and started trying to frame Jack, with Elizabeth Harvey colluding in the plan.' Archie lit a cigarette and exhaled a puff of smoke. 'I always thought Duncan was a strange fellow, but I never thought he was criminally devious. What do you think of the wife? Is she reliable? I don't want to go off half cock with a lot of wild accusations.'

'I believe we should investigate, sir,' interjected Frobisher. 'Mrs de Silva was convinced that Ella Duncan was genuinely frightened, but not out of her mind.'

Clutterbuck pondered a moment then nodded. 'Very well. We'll take it further.'

* * *

It was late afternoon when they reached the entrance to the Duncans' bungalow. As Archie's car rounded the first bend in the drive, the neglected rockery that de Silva had noticed on his previous visit came into view, rising up the slope towards the bungalow and separated from the drive by a wide gully. But it wasn't the sight of the jumble of rocks, overgrown with weeds and thuggish shrubs, that made Archie slam on the brakes; it was the sight of Ella Duncan running helter-skelter down the uneven stone steps that zigzagged through the rocks. She had reached a point nearly three-quarters of the way down to the lily pond at the bottom.

'Over there, on the steps!' Archie said. The car moved off as he put his foot down. 'That's Duncan's car on the drive,' he said when they crunched to a halt on the gravel sweep in front of the bungalow. 'But where's he got to?'

'I see him, sir.' Charlie Frobisher pointed to the top of the rockery steps where Duncan stood, apparently shouting something down to his wife. He must have been intent on what he was doing for he seemed not to notice their arrival.

'I doubt he's calling her up for a G&T,' said Archie with grim humour. 'We'd better intervene and quickly.'

Apparently still oblivious to their presence, Duncan started quickly down the uneven steps. He didn't look back when Archie shouted his name, but at the next turn in the way, he lost his footing. The three men watched as he stumbled and tried to right himself, but his weight must have dislodged the slab of stone forming the step on which he stood. With a cry, he overbalanced and fell, cracking his head on a jagged rock.

Charlie Frobisher started to run towards Duncan who staggered to stand upright, blood running down his face. But he fell once more and, as his skull struck rock, his head snapped sideways. This time he didn't get up.

Reaching him, Charlie Frobisher knelt at his side and grabbed him by the shoulders. De Silva scrambled down the steps as fast as he could with Archie in his wake.

'Is he alive?' he asked.

'I'm not sure.'

'We'd better not move him,' Archie broke in. 'Get up to the bungalow, Frobisher. Call Hebden and tell him to bring a nurse.' He glanced down the slope to where Ella Duncan was now huddled by the pond, her knees clasped to her chest and her face hidden. A strange keening sound floated up to them.

Gingerly, de Silva negotiated his way past Duncan's motionless body and went to help her. She raised her tear-stained face and stared confusedly at him.

'Are you hurt, ma'am?'

Feebly, she shook her head, but as he helped her up, he noticed that, close to her left eye, a red weal was rising rapidly, and blood was oozing from her split lower lip. Her hand went to cover it and she cried out in pain. 'I'm not sure if I can walk,' she gasped. De Silva helped her to the nearest step, and she sat down, then clutched the hem of his tunic. 'You will stay with me?' Her eyes widened with fear. 'You won't let him near me, promise me, please.'

De Silva realised that she hadn't fully understood what had happened. There was no point distressing her further. She held out her hands in a supplicant gesture and he enclosed them with his own. 'I promise.'

'He noticed I was on the telephone and wanted me to tell him who I was talking to, but I wouldn't. You won't make me tell him, will you?'

'Of course not, ma'am. No one will make you do anything you don't want to do.'

He scanned the rockery and noticed there was another way to the top that didn't involve passing Duncan's body. 'We'll take it slowly, ma'am,' he said, 'but only when you're ready, I'd like to help you back to the bungalow.'

* * *

'The blow must have dislocated the atlas vertebra from the occipital cranium,' said Hebden when he had examined Duncan's body.

'And what does that mean in plain English?' growled Archie irritably.

'The atlas vertebra is situated at the top of the spine where the spine joins the skull. It supports the head, hence the name, after the Greek god, Atlas, who supported the world on his shoulders.'

'Yes, yes; spare us the classical references, Hebden.'

Hebden coloured slightly and de Silva, who had handed Ella Duncan over to the care of the nurse and returned to the party, felt sorry for him. Archie was certainly in a foul mood. Perhaps he was thinking of how to avoid a scandal at his precious golf club and not coming up with any answers.

'In certain cases, a blow can result in internal decapitation,' Hebden went on stiffly. 'I believe that is what happened here.'

Archie drew a deep breath. 'Well, you'd better get on with moving the body. Where's Mrs Duncan?'

'Up at the bungalow with my nurse, I believe. I'll see to it she's cared for.'

'Good. The poor lady has had a most unpleasant experience. When the time's right, can I rely on your wife to offer her assistance, de Silva? I expect Mrs Clutterbuck will do her bit too.'

'I'll speak to her, sir. I'm sure Jane will be glad to help Mrs Duncan until she finds her feet again.' And her help might be more welcome than Florence's robust ministrations, he thought wryly.

CHAPTER 35

*A few weeks later – the day of Emerald Watson's
and David Hebden's wedding*

In the weeks that followed the death of Tom Duncan, a search of the Duncans' bungalow revealed copious notes in Tom Duncan's handwriting. There were dates, times and places; the earliest of them relating to the affair between his wife and Mark Brodie and the later ones to Mark Brodie's one with Elizabeth Harvey. There were also photographs of Brodie and more notes on his business affairs. It was as if Duncan had been building up a dossier of evidence.

Following Ella Duncan's revelations, the charge of murder against Mark Brodie had been dropped, but he and Elizabeth Harvey were still accused of conspiring to pervert the course of justice. They remained in Kandy until it was time for their trial. Ella was still in the care of Doctor Hebden, where Jane had visited her on several occasions and begun the slow process of winning her trust.

Thanks to Charlie Frobisher, the mystery of the Victoria Clinic had also been solved. Expecting Brodie to be busy at the club the whole of that Friday morning, Elizabeth Harvey had booked an appointment, but when she discovered he would still be able to meet her, she'd missed it and not bothered to cancel.

'Shanti?' Jane stopped in the middle of powdering her

face. A smattering of powder drifted from the swansdown puff onto the top of her dressing table.

'Mm?'

'I've been thinking. Suppose Brodie had chosen someone other than David Llewellyn for his alibi? Someone who stuck to their story?'

'Duncan would have had to cross that bridge when he came to it. Fortunately for him, Brodie did choose Llewellyn and he wasn't hard to catch out.'

'But Duncan couldn't have anticipated that Brodie would influence the owner of the Blue Cat into lying about when Jack left the club. He must have had some anxious moments when it looked as if Jack would be convicted. The owner of the club might have stuck to his story. No wonder he fought so hard to defend Jack.'

'Yes. It was also a piece of luck for him that Elizabeth Harvey's conscience pricked her into confessing.'

Jane resumed powdering her cheeks. 'Not just luck. I'm sure that by then, Duncan expected you to see through Brodie's tricks. You should be flattered.'

'I'm not sure his opinion of me was so high,' said de Silva with a smile. 'But thank you all the same, my love.'

Brushing a smattering of powder from the skirt of her royal blue dress, Jane stood up from the dressing table stool. She patted her hair. 'Does this look alright?'

'Why?'

She frowned with mock annoyance. 'What a question! You're supposed to say of course it does. It's a new style.'

'It looks lovely,' said de Silva hastily. He glanced at his watch. 'We'll be late if we don't set off in the next few minutes.'

'I'm ready.' She picked up her gloves. 'Oh and by the way, I forgot to tell you that I asked Emerald about that place, the Victoria Clinic. She didn't know anything, but she found out from David Hebden that despite all the white coats and flummery, they don't have any proper doctors there.'

De Silva's forehead creased. 'Then what do they do?'

'Very expensive beauty treatments and massages. Emerald and I thought we might investigate what they have to offer one day.'

'How could you possibly be made more beautiful, my love?' asked de Silva quickly. He'd already made one mistake.

Jane flicked his arm with her gloves. 'What nonsense you talk.'

As they drove to the church, he savoured the rushing of the wind in his face. It was wonderful to be free of the cares of work, with nothing to do except celebrate a very happy occasion.

Roses festooned the lychgate; the flower arrangers of Nuala had done the couple proud. More flowers decorated the church, filling the air with their scent. De Silva and Jane took their places a few rows behind the Clutterbucks. The Applebys, who had taken it upon themselves to stand in as family for Emerald ever since she decided to stay in Nuala, occupied the front pew on the other side. David Hebden sat at the end of their row, ready to come forward to meet his bride.

The joyous opening fanfare of Mendelssohn's wedding march rang through the church, and the buzz of chatter from the congregation hushed. Turning his head, de Silva saw Emerald enter on the arm of George Appleby, Emerald's friend Charlotte's husband. David Hebden rose in readiness.

'Doesn't she look beautiful?' whispered Jane. 'What a lovely couple they make, and what a perfect day.'

Reaching to squeeze her hand, de Silva thought how right she was. The fanfare gave way to the music's stately chords. All around him there were smiling faces.

Harmony was restored to Nuala. The rough time was over.